HANGMAN'S GOLD

SLATE•STEPHENS #2 M•Y•S•T•E•R•I•E•S

HANGMAN'S GOLD

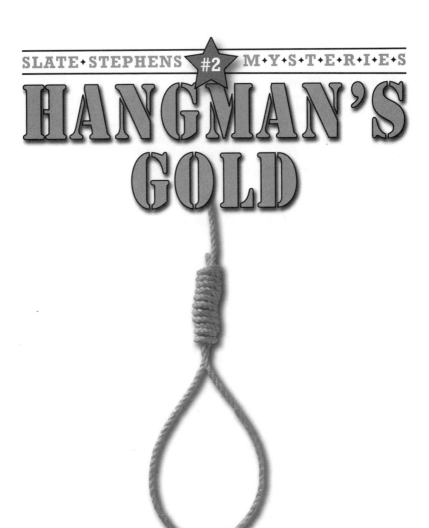

Sneed B. Collard III

www.buckinghorsebooks.com

Distributed by Mountain Press Publishing Company, Missoula, Montana
1-800-234-5308
www.mountain-press.com

Cover and Book Design by Kathleen Herlihy-Paoli, Inkstone Design.
The text of this book is set in New Century Schoolbook.
It is printed on 30% post-consumer waste paper.

Collard, Sneed B.
    Hangman's gold / by Sneed B. Collard III. -- 1st ed.
    p. cm. -- (Slate Stephens mysteries ; #2)
    SUMMARY: Twelve-year-old detectives Slate Stephens
    and Daphne McSweeney risk their lives to find lost gold
    from Montana's vigilante era while working to recover
    two priceless Charles Russell paintings stolen from a
    university art museum.
    LCCN 2011910923
    ISBN-13: 978-0-9844460-2-5
    ISBN-10: 0-9844460-2-8

    1. Gold--Juvenile fiction. 2. Art theft--
Investigation--Juvenile fiction. 3. Montana--Juvenile
fiction. 4. Detective and mystery stories. [1. Gold--
Fiction. 2. Art theft--Fiction. 3. Montana--Fiction.
4. Mystery and detective stories.] I. Title.
II. Series: Collard, Sneed B. Slate Stephens mysteries ; #2.

    PZ7.C67749Han 2011   [Fic]
                        QBI11-600138

Manufactured in the United States of America

10 9 8 7 6 5 4 3 2 1

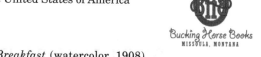

Image of *Bronc to Breakfast* (watercolor, 1908)
by Charles M. Russell courtesy of the Montana
Historical Society, Helena, Montana.

For Penny Collard,
Who embraces the mysteries of life.
Love, Sneed

One

"Butcher Dan, Bad-Luck MacIntyre, and Slippery Slate, the three of you have been tried by this vigilance committee. We find you guilty of the following crimes: murder, larceny, extortion, intimidation, and the use of foul language in front of respectable women. Before I read your sentence, how do you respond?"

Dan, one of the two men next to me, clears his throat and hawks out a fat glob of spit onto the frozen ground. "Ain't got nothin' to say to youse. None of youse got the right to judge us!"

Bad-Luck MacIntyre, the man standing between Dan and me, isn't so composed. His knees knock together. A steaming river of snot flows from his nose. "Please! I beg you! Allow me to go to my house and say g'bye to my sweet Martha 'n the kids! They got nobody 'round here. Just grant me one minute to say my farewells. You kin even keep my hands tied."

The man who pronounced our sentence—the Judge—looks back at the twenty other stone-faced men behind him. "Boys?" he asks.

"Let 'em swing," one of the men growls. "We're gettin' cold."

The Judge turns his eyes back to the man next

to me. "Sorry, Mac. Can't do it."

Finally, the Judge looks my way. "Slippery Slate Stephens, you have anything you want to tell us?"

Actually, I do. I want to protest my guilty verdict, demand a lawyer, and ask how I ended up here in the first place. Unfortunately, I am so petrified that my tongue sticks to my throat like a log to a dry creek bed.

The Judge waits an entire four seconds for me to answer, then moves on. "Very well. By order of this Court of Justice, we sentence the three of you to Death by hanging, to be carried out immediately."

The Executioner—a man as big as a slab of granite—steps up from behind us. With cracked, calloused hands, he fits nooses around each of our necks and snugs them down.

"Up on the barrels you three," he growls.

"No! This can't be happening!" my mind shouts, but again, the words can't find my tongue. One by one, we are boosted up onto the wooden barrels. The ropes are pulled tight over the log beam of the gallows above our heads.

The Judge asks us, "Any last words?"

Butcher Dan glares at the crowd before him. "I'll see you all in HELL!"

The Judge nods and the Executioner kicks the barrel out from under him. Dan is lucky. Even though the drop is short, it manages to break his neck, killing him instantly. Fortune does not shine *so brightly onto Bad-Luck Mac. He survives the drop, and is left strangling, his feet kicking wildly only inches above the frozen earth. His desperate, choking squeals send a fresh wave of terror through me and my legs almost collapse of their own accord.*

The Executioner lets out a harsh guffaw. "Now, now, Slippery Slate. No need to hurry yourself," he tells me. "We'll take care 'o you faster than a moose can poop."

The Executioner looks at the Judge. "Ready?"

The Judge nods.

"NO!" I finally manage to scream.

"Yes, sorry son. We've got to get moving."

My eyes snap open.

Instead of a group of stone-faced men, I see the pinkish light of dawn shining through the nylon wall of our tent.

"Too early," I moan, gophering back into my down sleeping bag.

Dad gives me a playful kick. "Slate, it's almost broad daylight. C'mon. Hot water is on, and we've got a lot of ground to cover before Len and Daphne arrive tonight."

That gets me moving. Not the hot water. Daphne's arrival. It's been almost two weeks since I've seen her. Our families had planned to stay in Helena the entire summer so that our dads could study the earthquake faults in the area. My father finished his part of the work early, though. While my mom and sister returned to Missoula, and Daphne and her family stayed in Montana's capital, Dad dragged me down here to the ghost town of Bannack to assist him on a last-minute consulting job—doing some prospecting for a large gold mining company.

"Get dressed," Dad instructs, leaving the tent and zipping the large flap behind him. "It's supposed to get up into the nineties today, and I want to beat the heat."

Eighteen minutes, a bowl of oatmeal, and a trip to the outhouse later, I am following my dad on a trail north, away from the deserted main street of Bannack. Within a couple hundred yards, we pass two tall posts with a log beam mounted on top of them. A shudder passes through me and I stop to stare at the gallows.

Dad also stops. "What's the matter?"

Our rush to get ready had made me forget about my nightmare, but now it lurches back to me in disturbing detail. "Uh," I tell him. "I had a bad dream last night."

Dad looks from me to the gallows and back again. He grins. "That book about the vigilantes getting to you? Perhaps you should read something else."

"That's all I could find," I say.

Still, as we continue past the gallows, I think, *Dad's right. I should dig up a less frightening book— maybe something about flesh-eating dinosaurs or parasitic aliens attacking earth.*

Two

Prospecting for gold isn't nearly as exciting as it sounds. I usually spend the entire day trudging after my father through sagebrush, up over hills, and down into ravines. Every once in a while, Dad stops, turns slowly in circles, and picks up a rock to examine. My job is to write down the things he tells me, use a hand-held GPS device to mark locations on a geological map, and collect rock samples until my pack is heavier than I am. Oh yeah, I'm also the "safety guy." I make sure that, in his frenzy to understand every rock and dirt clod in an area, my dad doesn't accidentally tumble down a mine shaft and kill himself.

Today, though, we manage to get back to our campsite before my dad does a header into a hole, and before my rock-filled pack drags me into the dirt. I have Len and Daphne to thank for that.

Even though Dad would like to hike the hills until midnight, he's also the King of Organization. He wants to make sure our camp is spic-and-span before Len and Daphne show up. By the time I spot the OFGOV—the Official Field Geology Operations Vehicle—rumbling down the gravel road toward us, our camp is so spotless a coyote wouldn't even sniff it.

"Slate!" Daphne shouts, leaping out of the Travelall's door even before Len has turned off the engine.

I have been thinking about this moment for the last two weeks, and have carefully planned how I would greet Daphne. After weighing every option, I concluded that a light punch on the shoulder would be most appropriate. Daphne, though, crashes into me and throws her arms around me.

Her option is better.

"Nice campsite," Len says, sauntering up to us.

Dad shakes hands with him. "Me and Cal, the campground manager, go way back."

"Is that Grasshopper Creek?" Daphne exclaims, looking at the cold, clear trout stream within spitting distance of our tent.

"Yeah," I tell her.

"This is great!" she shouts, twirling slowly, taking in the rugged valley and hills surrounding us.

Len and Dad both chuckle.

"What?" Daphne challenges them.

My dad waves his hand, still smiling. "No. No. You're absolutely right. This is great."

"Where do we put our tent?"

"I was thinking over there." Dad gestures to a clear patch of ground on the other side of the picnic table, next to a stand of cottonwoods.

"Why don't you and Slate set up the tent while Andrew and I unload the Travelall?" Len suggests.

"Well," I say, "I was kind of hoping to show Daphne a little of Bannack before it gets dark."

"Can we?" Daphne pleads.

Len and my dad look at each other and Len sighs like a stage actor. "Go ahead," he tells us. "As usual, we will do all your chores for you."

We don't bother responding to that insulting remark. Instead, Daphne grabs her camera and we practically skip out of the campground.

"How were the last two weeks in Helena?" I ask, my feet breezing down the dry gravel road. Just being so close to Daphne again, watching her struggle to keep black wisps of hair out of her face, fills my heart and body with emotional helium. I realize that I've missed her even more than I thought I did. Way more.

But before I totally float into the stratosphere, Daphne says, "The last two weeks were great."

And just like that, my spirits deflate.

"Oh."

Her response is not the one I want to hear. What I want to hear is how her longing for me plunged her into deepest, darkest despair.

"I got into Yearbook at school!" she exclaims. "And you are *never* going to believe this."

"What?" I whimper like a dog that's been kicked.

But before she can answer, the silent buildings of the ghost town stretch out ahead of us.

Daphne's shoes scrunch to a halt. "Wow."

I also stop and take in the old town. It is so awe-inspiring that I decide to rise above Daphne's soul-deflating remark about the last two weeks, and give her a second chance. After all, maybe she meant that her last two weeks were great *except* for missing me more than life itself. *Yeah,* I think. *That's probably it.*

Unaware of my mental debate, Daphne keeps her eyes fixed on the town. "It looks so authentic," she says.

I straighten up my posture, and say, "Yeah. Bannack isn't like Helena. When Bannack became a state park, they didn't try to make everything look new again. They just preserved the buildings as they were."

"Great light right now." Daphne lines up a picture with the late afternoon sun reflecting off the ancient buildings. She snaps the shot, checks it, then lowers her camera. "I like this place," she says.

"There used to be a lot more buildings," I tell her, showing off what I've learned in the past two weeks. "About 3,000 people lived in Bannack right after gold was discovered. Over time, most of the buildings got burned or torn down, but this one here is the Governor's Mansion." I point to a crooked, warped hovel made out of rough-cut wooden beams.

Daphne gives her cute little snort. "The Governor lived in that?"

"Well, remember, this was 1863, and he was only

the territorial governor. Montana hadn't become a state yet."

"What's that over there?" Daphne asks, gesturing to a cool-looking wooden structure with multi-pane windows across the front.

"That's the assay office. It's where the miners brought their gold to see how pure it was."

"Slate, I know what an assay office is. Hello? Our fathers are geologists?"

I blush. "Oh yeah."

Daphne smiles and then walks toward a two-story, weathered building with a chimney and bell-tower. "Isn't that the old school house and Masonic Lodge?"

I follow her toward it, puzzled. "How did you know that?"

"Oh, uh…" Daphne stammers. "I think I read something about it somewhere."

I halt. "Wait a minute. Have you been here before?"

Now it's Daphne's turn to blush. "Well, yes, but it was a long time ago."

Can I feel any more stupid? Here I am showing off how smart I am, and Daphne probably knows everything I've told her already. "Why didn't you tell me?" I demand.

"I don't know," she says. "You just seemed happy to be giving me the tour."

"Great," I huff, my mood again souring.

"Come on, Slate. I didn't know everything you told me."

"Only ninety percent? Ninety-nine-point-nine percent?"

"Don't take it that way. I liked hearing it from you. Let's keep going."

"Fine," I grunt, following as she resumes walking toward the building.

The schoolhouse/Masonic Lodge is surrounded by a weathered, gray picket fence and sagebrush bushes taller than I am. Still steaming, I push past Daphne and march up to the door. I jerk on the handle and the door squeaks open.

"Are we allowed to go in there?" Daphne asks.

Without answering, I step inside.

Believe it or not, I actually haven't been in that many of the buildings here in Bannack. Dad's kept me so busy, that I usually don't feel like exploring much after our days hiking around. Now, though, stepping inside Montana's first classroom, a shiver runs through me. Yellowish pull-down shades, the color of a dead person's skin, are drawn over the windows, and the low-angled sun casts an other-worldly glow over rows of wooden desks that have sat undisturbed for more than sixty years.

I hear the door squeak closed behind me. "This is eerie," Daphne whispers. "Look at those old chalk boards on the wall."

I nod silently. On the boards, someone has scrawled "Rules for Students 1872". They include:

* Respect your Schoolmaster. Obey and Respect their punishments.
* Do not call your Classmates names or fight with them.
* Never make noise or disturb your neighbors as they work.

And my personal favorite,

* Bring firewood into the classroom whenever the teacher tells you to.

"Geez, can you imagine going to school here?" Daphne asks. "Sitting at these desks for six or seven hours a day? It looks like teachers back then didn't put up with any wriggling around, either."

I slide into a hard, wooden chair attached to a desk.

"Slate, that's creepy," Daphne tells me. "I mean, everyone who used to sit in those seats is probably *dead*."

Of course, her comment only encourages me. I raise my hand and say, "Uh, Mrs. Teacher, I have to go to the outhouse! Really. It's Number Two and I have to go now!"

Daphne pulls back her lips into her irritated frog look. "You are so puerile, Slate."

Daphne and I like to throw tough vocabulary words at each other, and I have to admit that she's stumped me with 'puerile'. Before she can demand a definition, I ask, "I wonder if there's any gum still stuck under the desk?"

My ploy works. Daphne turns away in disgust as I feel around under the desk. I find nothing, so my hands reach down under the chair.

And that's when I touch it. Something jammed into a crack between the seat and the chair frame. Without thinking, I pull it out—a piece of wadded up paper.

"What's that?" Daphne says, stepping over to me.

"It was underneath the chair."

"And you removed it? Slate, this is a state park!"

"It's just an old piece of paper," I say, still miffed she didn't tell me she'd been to Bannack before. To prove my point, I slap the paper down on the desk, unroll it, and press it flat with my palm. At first I can't tell what I'm looking at. Then I let out a surprised "Huh!"

Daphne leans over so that a lock of her hair tickles my neck. "What is it?"

"It's a map," I say. "It looks like…a treasure map.

Three

"What?" Daphne exclaims, seizing the paper. "Hey, that's mine!" I tell her, standing up so fast my hip bangs against the side of the school desk.

"This isn't much of a map," Daphne says, studying it.

"Don't be so literal. It's a *metaphorical* map," I say, throwing my own vocabulary word at her.

But Daphne is right. Even though there's a little sketch showing Bannack and the gallows, the important thing is a poem, or riddle, below it.

Daphne reads the ornate, curving script:

From the place of Plummer's demise,
Walk to town to seek your prize.

A yellow journal points you to
The location of your second clue.

If your thoughts fall into line,
You'll recognize Our Dear Lord's prime.

To a House Divided, take this mark,
And count to how a wolf is cloaked.

And with that precious knowledge stored,
Find the dwelling of one once adored.

Of its bricks take proper stock,
And pace them down a Confederate walk.

A lucky one will dig with pleasure,
To claim the vigilantes' treasure.

She lowers the riddle and looks at me. "Does any of this make sense to you?"

I repossess *my* piece of paper and read it again. "A little. But I'm not sure I should tell *you*."

Daphne sinks her fingers into my ribs. "Slate, tell!"

I leap back with a yelp. "Okay! Okay! Let's go outside. This room gives me the creeps."

Out in front of the schoolhouse sits an old-fashioned merry-go-round—one shaped like a hexagon, with six wooden boards to sit on. We plonk down on it facing out, and begin pushing ourselves in lazy circles with our feet. The first hints of chilly night air tickle my skin and to the west, we see the golden rays of the setting sun slice through willow and cottonwood trees.

Daphne scoots close so that our shoulders are touching. "So what is this talking about?"

"Uh…" After two weeks of not seeing Daphne, the feel of her warm shoulder against mine sidetracks my attention from the piece of paper, and I forget all about being mad at her earlier. It might be different if she and I had been boyfriend/girlfriend forever, but that's not the case. Even though we've been friends for years, we only admitted that we liked each other a few weeks ago—before my dad brought me down to Bannack. Since then, all I've really thought about is—

"Slate?" Daphne nudges me. "The paper?"

"Oh, yeah." I force myself to focus on the riddle in my hands. "Uh, most of this doesn't make any sense, but…"

"But what?"

I study the words more carefully. "I think the first and last lines do."

"You mean 'From the place of Plummer's demise?'"

I nod. "Yeah. I've been reading about him in this book about the vigilantes. Henry Plummer was the first sheriff of Bannack. He was very popular and got himself elected sheriff less than a year after gold was discovered here."

"What happened to him? Did some bad guys gun him down here on Main Street?"

I give a little grunt. "No. That would have been heroic. What really happened is that a bunch of robberies and a few murders took place in the area. After a while, people got suspicious that their own sheriff was in charge of the gang of outlaws doing them."

"Oh, that's right!" Daphne exclaims. "We studied

that in school. And that's when all the honest citizens formed a vigilante movement and hanged all the bad guys—including Sheriff Plummer, right?"

"Well, yeah, sort of," I tell her. "They did hang Plummer—on the gallows right up there," I say, pointing to the gulch north of town. "But the book makes the whole vigilante movement seem more complicated than that."

"How?" Daphne hooks a strand of her black hair over her ear and a familiar feeling hits me. It's as if cool spring water suddenly surges up through my body, making my heart swim like an excited trout inside my chest cavity.

"Uh..." I stammer again, lost in Daphne's hazel eyes.

"Slate," she prods me with a smile.

"Oh, right. Um, so this book I was reading said that there really wasn't that much proof against Plummer. He might have been involved in the robberies, but some of the vigilantes may have just wanted to get rid of him for political reasons. This was during the Civil War, and Plummer was a Democrat and a friend of ordinary miners. Most of the vigilantes were wealthy Republicans, and some may have felt Plummer was working against their interests."

"Are you saying Plummer might have been innocent?"

I shrug. "No one will ever know. The vigilantes

didn't hold a trial. They just took him out and lynched him—along with several dozen other people. In fact, Montana had the largest vigilante movement anywhere in the United States. Between 1864 and 1870, vigilantes murdered almost sixty people."

"*Murdered?* I thought the people they hanged were bad guys?"

"Some of them were. But this book I read said it's pretty clear they also hanged some people just because they didn't like them *hanging around.*"

Daphne punches me in the shoulder. "Slate, that was terrible."

I grin. "Couldn't resist."

"Anyway," Daphne continues. "You're saying the vigilantes were actually bad guys?"

I again shrug. "It depends on how you look at it. Did they get rid of some criminals? Yeah. Were they criminals themselves? Yeah, because they killed people without holding legal trials. It was a bad situation."

Daphne leans across me and points to the piece of paper.

"Well, what do these last two lines mean, 'A lucky one will dig with pleasure, and claim the vigilantes' treasure?' What treasure are they talking about?"

I slowly shake my head. "Hm...I don't know, unless..."

Daphne nudges me. "Unless what?"

I suddenly breathe in the scent of Daphne's peach

shampoo and my head spins, driving off whatever hint of an idea might have been flitting through my mind. I look at Daphne and want to kiss her. Shoot, I've wanted to kiss her all summer! But as my body sways toward her, panic grips me. My joints lock, my saliva glands dry up, and for the hundredth time, I chicken out.

Instead of kissing her, I swallow hard and croak, "It's getting dark. Maybe our dads have dinner ready."

Four

Dad One and Dad Two do indeed have dinner prepared by the time we return to camp. Between eating, cleaning up, and getting the other tent ready, Daphne and I don't get a chance to talk any more about the treasure map and riddle. Before I go to sleep, though, I do pull out the vigilante book I've been reading and, by the light of my mini-flashlight, skim the last few chapters.

The next morning, Dad again kicks me awake in my sleeping bag just as dawn breaks. Daphne and Len are already up, hovering around the cook stove.

"Good morning," Daphne brightly greets me.

"Is it?" I grunt. In case you haven't figured it out, I am not a morning person.

"Can I have some coffee?" I ask Dad.

He's always said no in the past, but today, he surprises me and hands me his cup.

"Just one drink—and don't tell Mom."

"I won't," I say, raising the mug to my lips. I take a little sip and it's all I can do to keep from spitting it onto the ground. How can adults drink this stuff—especially without sugar and milk in it? It's like drinking paint thinner or jet fuel. With Daphne's hazel eyes on me, however, I force down the black, bitter brew and pretend I'm the coolest dude in the world, having my morning cuppa joe.

After breakfast, the four of us climb into the OFGOV, and bump and rumble along dirt roads as if we're in a stagecoach. Dad drives us to a new area he and Len want to prospect. After piling out of the Travelall, we wriggle into our daypacks and follow a trail through a beautiful area of mixed pine forest. But if there's one thing geologists hate, it's trails. In no time, Dad leaves the path and plunges down a long draw filled with sagebrush and dried cow patties. Finally, I feel fully awake.

"So," I ask Daphne, "you were going to tell me some news yesterday."

Daphne looks confused.

"You know," I prompt. "You said I wasn't going to believe it."

Daphne's smile flashes in the morning light. "Oh yeah! Our *Highlights* article! They're going to take it!"

I stumble over a gnarled sage stump. "No way! How much are they going to pay us? A thousand dollars? Ten thousand?"

"They didn't say. And they said we need to revise it first."

I sputter, "*Revise?* What's wrong with it? It seemed perfect to me."

"Oh, please, Slate," she tells me. "All writers have to revise their work. We're lucky they even want it."

I grunt, but really am pleased. And for those of you who don't know what I'm talking about, let me back up a little.

Earlier in the summer, when Daphne and I were both in Helena with our families, the governor of Montana lost his dog, a Border collie named Cat. Well, he didn't lose Cat exactly. Cat simply disappeared, and Daphne and I decided to use our super-sleuthing skills to try to find him. It took us about a week, but we finally figured out what had happened and, with a little help, returned Cat to the Capitol.

After Daphne and I found Governor Rickson's dog, we were bombarded by newspaper, T.V., radio, and blog requests. Then we got a surprise letter from the editor of the magazine *Highlights for Children*. She told us that she would love it if we wrote a story about how we figured out what happened to Cat— and, of course, about how we almost got eaten by a grizzly bear while doing it. Before my dad dragged me down here to Bannack, Daphne and I worked on the story almost every day. Then we finally sent it in. I guess I didn't really expect to hear from them, but it just shows you that when you think you've got it all figured out, life can surprise you.

"When are they going to publish our article?" I ask Daphne.

"After we send in the revision, I suppose."

"Do we need an agent—you know, to negotiate the movie rights, that sort of thing?"

Daphne rolls her eyes. "Right. And we'd better pick out our clothes for the Academy Awards while we're at it."

"I want to wear one of those shiny gold tuxedos."

"I don't care what I wear—as long as I'm walking next to someone cute."

"Oh, you mean *me*, of course."

Daphne and I look at each other and both burst out laughing.

Right then, Dad and Len stop to discuss granite intrusions and ore bodies—more on that later. I seize the opportunity to talk with Daphne in private.

I stroll ten or fifteen yards away and motion Daphne to follow. "Daphne," I say, my voice low. "I think I figured out what that message is about."

Daphne's eyes flare. "You mean about the vigilante's treasure?"

I quickly glance at our dads to make sure they are still locked in geology talk.

"Yeah," I answer. "I found something in my vigilante book last night. In the second-to-the-last chapter, it said that people have always *speculated*—that means to guess based on a—"

Daphne again punches me in the shoulder. "I know what speculated means, dufus. Just tell me the story."

I try to not to grin. "Okay. What they said was that when the vigilantes hanged somebody, they took all of that person's gold."

"That's not very nice!"

"No one could ever prove it," I continue, "but there were a lot of rumors. And, here's the best part."

"What?"

"The gold has never been recovered!"

"Slate, Daphne, let's go," Len calls. The dads move out, continuing down the valley, and Daphne and I follow, hanging back to stay out of earshot.

"But you said it was just a rumor," Daphne says. "It might not really be true."

"Yeah, but don't you see?" I say, barely able to keep my voice down. "Why would there be clues to a treasure that doesn't exist?"

Daphne tugs on her backpack's shoulder straps to tighten them. "But anyone could have made up a map or a riddle like that."

"Why?" I ask her. "What would be the point?"

"I...don't know. It's just that..."

"It's just that there *is* no point unless the treasure is really out there somewhere."

"But why would the clues be jammed under a desk in the school?"

I hop over some rabbit bush. "How should I know? Maybe one of the school kids found it. Or maybe one of the vigilantes figured no one would ever look for it there."

"I don't know, Slate. Sounds pretty *implausible*. That means it's not very likely," she says, trying to bait me.

"Very funny. But it's not im-plau-si-ble to me. It makes perfect sense."

"I suppose you're going to tell me next that you want me to help you find this treasure?"

"Well, duh! If it's there, we have as much right to it as anyone else. Besides, what have we got to lose?"

Even as I'm saying this, I am remembering uttering the exact same words—right before Daphne and I almost got killed by a grizzly bear up in Glacier Park. I am sure that Daphne is remembering, too.

Still, she looks at me, a spark in her eye. "I guess it's worth a try."

"That's what I'm saying! And, if we're right, we might make ourselves *rich*."

Five

Dad and Len spend the rest of the day trying to map the granite intrusion underground. It's not an easy task. The geology of this part of Montana is super complicated. Continental collisions, ocean sediments, erosion, volcanoes, and earthquakes have all created a landscape that is a thousand times more complex than the hardest jigsaw puzzle—which is exactly why my dad and Len love it.

To find gold, though, geologists have to look for very specific clues. Gold gets concentrated by big hot slabs of molten granite—called *granite intrusions*—pushing up into the earth's crust from deep underground.

"At high temperatures," my dad is always explaining to his college students, "the gold goes into solution. Hot steam from the granite carries gold and other minerals up toward the surface. As this steam reaches cooler rocks above, it cools down and the metals start precipitating out of it. Molybdenum—try saying that three times in a row—comes out first. Then iron, nickel, manganese, copper, and finally, gold. Gold and silica solidify at about the same temperature—which is why you often find gold inside of veins of quartz."

Not all of the gold is found in quartz, of course. Gold ore often just looks like orange or brown rock. Dad's job is to try to guess where concentrations of the gold ore might be, based on the geology of the area. If he thinks there might be some good gold deposits somewhere, he can tell the mining company. Then, they'll come in and dig some test holes, analyze the ore, and decide if it's worth it to set up mining operations.

By the end of a day following Dad One and Dad Two around—and listening to their endless discussions about rock formations and earthquake faults—Daphne and I are exhausted. However, we're not too exhausted to do a little gold prospecting of our own.

"We're going to go into Bannack," I announce as the OFGOV pulls back into our campsite.

Dad and Len raise eyebrows at each other, probably thinking "We've got to work these kids harder tomorrow."

Whereas our moms might have said no, however, the dads cave to our announcement like wet papier mache.

"Be back before dark," Len says.

"We will," Daphne replies with her convincing smile.

We hurry to the ghost town. A few cars—like grazing cows grabbing last mouthfuls of grass—remain in the visitor's parking lot, and I spot one couple strolling down near the far end of Main Street, taking pictures of the old church. Daphne and I turn left, however, and walk up Hangman's Gulch to the gallows.

While I remove the treasure map/riddle from my pocket, Daphne stares up at the solitary log beam fifteen feet above us. "Are these the actual gallows they hanged the bad guys from?"

"I don't think so," I tell her. "I overheard a park ranger explaining that after the vigilantes hanged Plummer and a bunch of other guys, one local drunk worried that he might be next in line. To keep that from happening, he staggered up here one night and chopped the gallows down. They did put up these replacement gallows in the exact same spot, however—the exact spot where Sheriff Plummer was hanged with two of his deputies."

Daphne and I both silently stare at the grisly landmark. Then, Daphne steps over to me and says, "So what do we have here?"

Together, we look at the piece of paper. We closely study the little sketch on it, but it's so, well, *sketchy*, that we again conclude that it's not important.

That leaves us with the riddle. Daphne again reads it out loud.

From the place of Plummer's demise,
Walk to town to seek your prize.

A yellow journal points you to
The location of your second clue.

If your thoughts fall into line,
You'll recognize Our Dear Lord's prime.

To a House Divided, take this mark,
And count to how a wolf is cloaked.

And with that precious knowledge stored,
Find the dwelling of one once adored.

Of its bricks take proper stock,
And pace them down a Confederate walk.

A lucky one will dig with pleasure,
To claim the vigilantes' treasure.

After she's finished, Daphne says, "Well, this looks like the right starting point. I guess we need to walk back into town."

I reach for her arm. "Wait a minute. Maybe we can skip these first few lines. Look down here."

"Down where?"

I point to the last three stanzas of the riddle. "See? It says, 'Find the dwelling of one once adored'?"

"So?" Daphne asks. "That could mean almost anyone."

"No, it couldn't. In my vigilante book, it goes on and on about how much everyone liked Henry Plummer when he first arrived in Bannack. That's why they elected him sheriff in the first place."

"Slate," Daphne says, "that's totally too easy. If they meant Sheriff Plummer's house, why would they bother writing all of the clues before it?"

"Maybe they weren't very smart," I say.

Daphne gives me her irritated frog face. "Maybe *you're* not too smart."

"Ha. Ha. Come on," I tell her. "I'm sure I'm right about this one. It'll save us a ton of time."

Daphne exhales noisily. "Do you know where Sheriff Plummer's house is?"

"Not exactly. But I know how we can find out."

Six

Near the entrance to Main Street is a visitor's center with a nice little bookstore inside. The store has already closed, but nearby sits a kiosk that contains self-guided brochures to Bannack. I remove one of the brochures and open it to a map showing all of Main Street, with each surviving building numbered and identified.

"I don't see Henry Plummer's house listed," Daphne tells me, looking over my shoulder.

"Me either. Maybe it's under one of the descriptions of the buildings."

Along with the map, the brochure contains pictures and descriptions of each remaining building in Bannack. Daphne pulls out her own copy so we can get through it faster, but after five minutes, she slaps the booklet closed. "Nothing."

"Shoot. Me either."

As I look up from the brochure, though, I recognize a familiar face walking our way. The woman wears a park uniform and a silver name tag reading "Arlis".

"Park's closed," she tells us in a stern voice.

"It's okay," I say. "We're only here to steal ancient artifacts."

Daphne looks at me in alarm.

Arlis smiles and asks, "How are you both, today?"

"Great. This is my friend Daphne."

Arlis shakes Daphne's hand. "Nice to meet you, Daphne. Welcome to Bannack. I'm the tour guide around here."

"Oh." Daphne releases Arlis's hand, then punches me in the shoulder. "Very funny, Slate."

Daphne is punching me so often I'm starting to get a bruise, but I grin and take it like a man.

To Arlis, Daphne says, "Nice to meet you, too."

"Daphne's dad is working with mine," I explain. "At least for a little while before school starts."

"Well," the tour guide says, sweeping her hand across the landscape. "You should find plenty to keep you occupied here."

I exchange a glance with Daphne thinking, *That's an understatement.*

"Can I help you find something?"

I am startled by the question and wonder if Arlis is reading our minds. Then she nods to the brochures Daphne and I are holding.

"Oh," I recover. "Yeah, maybe. We were just looking for Henry Plummer's house."

"We didn't find it on the map," Daphne fills in.

"That's because neither of the places where he lived survive," Arlis informs us.

"Can you tell us where it—they—used to be?" I ask.

"Well, before Plummer got married, he lived in a cabin up near Bachelor's row, not far from the gallows. That cabin was destroyed long ago. When the vigilantes arrested him, he was living with his wife's sister's family, the Vails, over on Yankee flats. Nothing survives over there either.

"Oh." Disappointment fills my voice.

We stand there silently for a moment. Then Daphne asks, "You don't happen to know if either of those buildings were made of brick, do you?"

Arlis smiles. "That, I can help you with. Almost all of the buildings in Bannack were made out of wood. The only brick building in town was the County Court House."

She points down the street to an impressive, two-story building that I've explored several times.

"Of course later," Arlis continues, "when the county seat got moved over to Dillon, the court house got turned into the Hotel Meade. Other than that, I don't know of any brick buildings in town."

"Okay. Thanks," I say.

Arlis bids us goodnight and heads out to her car in the parking lot.

"Now what?" I ask Daphne.

"Well, if you really want to do this, we need to start at the beginning—like I told you before. Read the first couple of lines again."

I pull out the riddle and read:

From the place of Plummer's demise,
Walk to town to seek your prize.

A yellow journal points you to,
The location of your second clue.

"So," Daphne says, "we need to look for a yellow journal. That mean anything to you?"

I shake my head. "Do you think they mean a notebook? Like a diary?"

Daphne and I begin walking down Main Street, pondering the silent buildings surrounding us. The town has totally emptied by now, and not for the first time, a strange feeling creeps over me. It's something I've felt only here in Bannack. It really is like I'm stepping into the past, but it's more than that. I almost feel like, well, all the people who used to live here are watching me. Not in a mean or scary way, but like they are glad to have some company after all this time.

Daphne must feel it, too. She moves closer and takes my hand as we walk. It's the first time we've held hands since I left Helena, and my heart thunders almost loud enough to echo off the surrounding hills.

"Wow," she says, forgetting about the clues. "This place is really something, isn't it?"

I nod. Now, though, I am thinking more about Daphne than about Bannack.

Finally, I decide that it's time for me to call up all of my courage and do what I've wanted to do for more than a month. Kiss Daphne.

I stop and turn to her. Daphne also turns and gazes at me with her jade-colored eyes.

I close my own eyes and start to lean toward her. My heart pounds like a rock crusher. My lips twitch, anticipating the Moment of Contact. Three... two...one...

"A newspaper!"

My eyes snap open.

"Huh?"

"A newspaper," Daphne repeats. "A journal could be a newspaper."

"Uh, I guess so," I mutter, reeling back from my cancelled kiss.

"In fact, didn't we learn about 'yellow journalism' in history class?"

It doesn't ring a bell for me. Then again, I've still got other bells ringing in my head. I was *so close* to finally kissing her, darn it! Even worse, I'm not sure I'll ever muster enough nerve to try again.

Daphne takes no notice of my distress. Either that, or she doesn't actually *want* to kiss me.

She continues, "You remember, Slate. Yellow journalism was when newspapers would come up with sensational headlines to force the government into doing something they wanted."

"Uh-huh." I still have no idea what she is talking about.

"William Randolph Hearst was the most famous yellow journalist. He whipped up all of these headlines to force us into declaring war on Spain back in the late 1890s."

"Why would he do that?"

"To sell more newspapers."

"But the Spanish American War happened a long time after the vigilantes hanged people. What could that have to do with here?"

Daphne scrunches her lips to the side and looks up and down the street. "I don't know, but the dads might be wondering about us. We'd better get back to the campground."

I don't know what I'm more disappointed about—not understanding the clue or not kissing Daphne. It doesn't matter. Shoulders slumped, I skulk with her back toward our campsite—and we do *not* hold hands.

Seven

The next day Dad—the Human Alarm Clock—kicks me awake at the usual too-early-for-anyone-to-be-awake time. This morning, though, we do not eat breakfast or drink bitter black coffee. We pile into the OFGOV and head out to the highway.

"We're not going prospecting today?" Daphne asks. She sits at the other end of the forward bench seat from me, a large gap between us.

I don't say anything. I am still waking up—and still sulking.

"Nope," Len answers Daphne. "We're short on supplies and thought we'd head into Dillon for breakfast."

"Cool!" Daphne exclaims.

"Whoopee," I mumble.

To reach Dillon, we drive over Badger Pass on Highway 278 and then descend through irrigated farmland populated by more than a hundred grazing pronghorn antelope. A half-hour later, Len parks next to a restaurant called Sparky's Garage, right across from the campus of the University of Montana Western.

Sparky's wakes me up a bit, and energizes my

mood. The restaurant has cashed in on America's nostalgia craze and is loaded with fun automobile memorabilia. The waitress seats us at a booth next to the window, and Daphne and I immediately begin studying the cool signs, license plates, and other stuff hanging from the walls and ceilings.

"Look," I say, pointing to a long metal sign. "'Pepsi-Cola, 5 cents. More Bounce to the Ounce.'"

"More Bounce to the Ounce!" Len exclaims. "Wasn't that the name of a techno funk tune?"

Daphne elbows him. "Dad, you are so *old*. Look at that sign over there, Slate. What on earth are Mola's O Cakes?"

I look at my own father, but he shakes his head. "Don't ask me. Never heard of them. Since we've already established that Len is so old, maybe you should ask him."

Len, who is actually a couple years younger than my dad, lets out a hearty laugh and says, "If I were you, Professor Stephens, I wouldn't be throwing rocks in my glass house!"

The waitress brings us utensils wrapped in red oil rags instead of napkins, and we all order breakfast. While we're waiting for our food, Dad and Len both call home. One problem with Bannack—or maybe it's an advantage—is that it's out of cell phone range. This is the first time in several days we've been able to check in with Stephens Family Headquarters back in Missoula. After talking to

Mom, Dad hands the phone to me and I answer all the usual questions:

"Are you having fun?"

"Are you eating enough?"

"Are you looking forward to school?"

"Is it nice having Daphne there?"

You know the drill. When I've finished being interrogated, Mom turns her phone over to my three year-old sister.

"Sate!" Lily shouts into the phone. "Are you coming home?"

I move the receiver a couple of inches away from my ear. "Not right now," I tell her.

"When?"

"Maybe in a couple of weeks."

"Will you be here for my birthday party?"

"Your birthday isn't until December, Lily."

"I'm going to be four!"

I laugh. "I *know*."

Just then, our food arrives.

"I've got to go, Lily. Tell Mom goodbye. Love you."

"I love you too, Sate."

We all dive into heaping plates of eggs, bacon, pancakes, and biscuits.

"Wow, this is good," I say, using a biscuit to shove a pile of eggs further into my mouth.

"Are you saying you're tired of instant oatmeal?" Dad teases.

Before I can answer, the air outside is shattered

by the loud wail of sirens. Everyone in the restaurant stops eating and stares as three police cars roar to a stop across the street. The officers jump out and race into a brick building that's part of the University of Montana Western.

"What do you suppose is going on?" Len asks.

In the booth next to us, we hear someone say, "They're going into the art museum."

Daphne and I are just finishing mopping up our breakfast.

"Can we go see what's happening?" I ask.

"No," Dad tells us. "There might be a shootout in progress."

We keep watching, though, and a moment later, a couple of the police officers emerge from the building, guns holstered, relaxed as licorice.

"Now can we go?"

Our mothers would definitely say no, but Dad and Len look at each other and shrug.

"Len and I will finish up and pay the bill," Dad tells us, "but stay at least fifty feet away from the police and don't interfere with them."

"Watch out for traffic, too," Len warns.

"It's a parking lot, Dad," chides Daphne.

"Well, then stay here," he counters.

"We'll watch for traffic," I assure him, and quickly scoot out of the booth.

Eight

By the time Daphne and I cross the street to the art museum, a local television news crew is setting up their equipment. A small crowd has formed and the police are stringing up a barrier of yellow tape that reads "Crime Scene—Do Not Cross!"

"What's going on?" I ask a man standing nearby.

"Someone broke into the art museum," he tells us.

"Did they steal anything valuable?"

The man shakes his head. "I don't know."

We notice the film crew moving in on the officer in charge, and Daphne tugs on my arm. "C'mon. Let's get closer so we can hear."

"Chief Bertek," asks a smartly-dressed blonde female reporter, "what can you tell us about the art museum break-in?"

The officer, who evidently heads up the Dillon Police Department, looks like he's been answering questions like this for the last fifty years. Holding a Styrofoam cup of coffee in one hand, he talks casually, as if he's discussing the upcoming UM Western football season. "Well, at approximately 6:30 a.m. this morning, the museum curator surprised a man armed with a small caliber weapon in the process of burglarizing the museum gallery."

"Was the curator harmed?"

"Fortunately not. But the burglar did tie him up before fleeing in a late model car."

"Could the curator identify the man?"

"Unfortunately, no. He was wearing a black ski mask. From the curator's description, though, the man was about five-foot ten inches and approximately 180 pounds."

"Can you tell us what, if anything, was stolen?" the reporter asks.

Chief Bertek takes a sip of coffee and then nods. "So far, it looks as if at least a dozen pieces are missing, including two valuable paintings by Charlie Russell."

Daphne and I gape at each other. Russell is not only Montana's most famous artist, but is known worldwide for his realistic paintings and sculptures about the Western frontier.

"Any idea who could have done this?" the reporter asks.

"We can't say at this time."

"Could it have been an inside job?"

"Again, we are still piecing together the evidence," Chief Bertek patiently answers. "But the Highway Patrol has set up checkpoints on all major roads leading into and out of the area. We would also welcome hearing from any members of the public who might have information regarding this crime."

With all of the excitement about the art museum heist, Daphne and I forget about the vigilantes' treasure until we've run all our errands in Dillon and returned to the campground in Bannack. By then, it's too late for the dads to drag us back into the field, so we're rewarded with an afternoon off. Clues in hand, we decide to walk down the dirt road to Bannack. At the entrance, we again review the riddle.

"So, where were we?" Daphne asks, looking at the paper in my hands. "Yellow journalism, right?"

My mind is already churning. "Yeah."

"I was thinking," Daphne says. "Just because yellow journalism didn't really take off until around 1900, that doesn't mean it couldn't be one of the clues. I mean, these clues could have been written many years after the vigilantes' activities, right?"

Suddenly, I slap my forehead. "Oh! I am so dumb!"

Daphne elbows me and grins. "You said it, not me."

"No!" I stammer impatiently. "This clue doesn't have anything to do with yellow journalism. Follow me!"

Grabbing Daphne's arm, I lead her to the first unlocked house we come to. Arlis and the other State Parks people leave most of the buildings unlocked so visitors can go in and out at will. Some of them are pretty creepy, too, with sagging, stained ceilings and old, moldy wallpaper peeling off the walls.

"Geez," Daphne says, as we enter the house. "I wouldn't want to live in here."

"Well, it probably used to be a lot nicer."

The house is one I've been in before. It is made of rough-hewn boards and the interior has a musty smell. If I had to guess, I'd say it's the fragrance of mold, mouse droppings, and body odor from miners who bathed only twice a year. Right now, though, I don't care how the house smells. I walk over to a wall and say, "Look."

Daphne steps closer. She studies the wall for a moment, then turns her green eyes to me in amazement. "Yellow journalism!"

Peeling off of the wall are long strips of old wallpaper, decorated with faded roses. Underneath the wallpaper are tacked sheet after sheet of old, yellowed newspapers.

I read the date on one of them. "February 1st, 1903."

"They must have used them as insulation," I say, noticing sunlight showing between the rough-cut beams of the house.

With her index finger, Daphne presses down the tip of her nose in thought. "They probably helped make a smoother surface to put the wallpaper on, too. But do you really think this is what the riddle is talking about?"

"What else could it be?"

"I concur," Daphne says, adopting her serious sleuthing voice. Then, she starts reading the headlines and articles on the newspapers. "But I don't see anything that could be a clue, do you? What's the next line of the riddle?"

I open our clues and read all three first stanzas:

> *From the place of Plummer's demise,*
> *Walk to town to seek your prize.*
>
> *A yellow journal points you to*
> *The location of your second clue.*
>
> *If your thoughts fall into line,*
> *You'll recognize Our Dear Lord's prime.*

"Big help," Daphne mutters.

"But," I tell her. "This isn't the only building with newspapers on the walls. All we have to do is find the right newspaper in the right building."

Nine

We spend the next hour scouring Bannack's buildings one by one. In several, we find old newspapers tacked to the walls, but none of the stories or advertisements on them jump out as clues.

"How do we even know what we're looking for?" Daphne finally asks.

I shake my head. "Don't know, but it must be a name or a news story about the vigilantes or something."

"What if we don't recognize it?"

In case you haven't noticed by now, Daphne isn't exactly comfortable with uncertainty. She's the GWTP—the Girl With The Plan. Fortunately, she's got me with her to help her improvise and go with the flow.

"We'll recognize it," I assure her.

By now, we have worked our way down to one of my favorite houses, the Roe/Graves House. The main reason I like it so much is that it's about the only place in Bannack I can actually imagine living in. A few nice trees and shrubs grow in the yard, surrounded by an old weathered picket fence. Time has stained the exterior of the building an attractive

Old West brown color, and the house looks a lot sturdier than most of the other buildings.

"What about here?" I ask Daphne as we enter the building. "Could you live in this place?"

Daphne surveys the almost empty living room. Right away, it is evident that this house has been better preserved inside than the others we have looked through.

"Maybe I could live here," Daphne replies, "if the choice was between here and a cave. And if this place had a hot tub."

I open the brochure I brought along. "No mention of a hot tub," I tell her, "but it does say that the house was built by William Roe and was one of the first frame houses built in Bannack. It also says that Roe made his money from shipping in and selling goods, and from banking."

Daphne snorts. "No surprise. It seems like that's how most of the real fortunes were made back then. Not by the guys who found the gold, but by the businessmen who sold them things. I remember reading in school about how Levi Strauss moved out West from New York City during the California Gold Rush. He wasn't interested in gold mining, but struck it rich making jeans for the miners."

I pluck a few loose hairs from my eyebrows. "Yeah," I mutter, my mind returning to the search for clues.

While Daphne walks into the large kitchen on

the left, I enter one of the back rooms and halt.

"Daphne, come here!"

She rushes in. "Did you find something?"

"I think so."

On the wall in front of me, strips of wallpaper have peeled away to reveal several full sheets of old newsprint. I point to one of them. "Look."

Near the top of the wall is an article with the headline reading "Bannack Newcomers Welcome at Gibson House." Daphne and I read through the article, which is dated 1891. I see that it's mostly a fluff piece, talking about how the Gibson family recently purchased a building that used to be called the Montana Hotel. The article states that the Gibsons are still running the place as a boarding house.

Daphne hooks a strand of her black hair behind an ear. "You think this is a clue?"

"I haven't seen any other possibilities, have you?"

"Not really, but why would it be this newspaper located in this house?"

My eyes return to the brochure entry on the Roe/ Graves house that we're standing in. "Well, look," I point. "Besides making it rich in Bannack, it says that William Roe was one of the original vigilantes that hanged Sheriff Plummer and his two deputies."

"Weren't there, like, a hundred vigilantes?" Daphne challenges me.

"Fifty to seventy-five according to the book I read.

But this all makes sense. This is the only article we've seen that refers to anything here in Bannack."

Daphne twists her lips to the side. "I guess you might be right."

I'm too excited to let Daphne's skepticism slow me down. "I *am* right. Let's go to the Gibson House to find our next clue!"

Taking Daphne by the hand, I tug her back outside and we cross the street to a wooden two-story house with the number 20 posted on a marker in front of it. Unfortunately, there's a padlock on the door.

"Darn," Daphne says.

I flip the brochure back open and read the entry on the Gibson House. Correction. Make that the Gibson *Houses*.

"Oh," I tell Daphne. "The house next door also belonged to the Gibsons. C'mon!"

We walk to a single-story house next to the rooming house and push open the door.

"Weird," Daphne says.

"You can say that again."

"Weird."

I ignore Daphne's anemic attempt at humor, because in front of us is something I never would have expected. The entire eastern wall of the room we are standing in is built of exposed, rough-cut logs. That's not the surprising part. What's surprising is that the wall has been branded with hundreds of symbols, numbers, letters, and shapes.

"What happened here?" Daphne asks. "Do you think the Gibsons let their kids burn designs into the walls? You know, 'Kids, since there's nothing on television tonight, you just fire up the furnace and burn some more brands into the wall to keep yourselves busy.'"

I do laugh this time, but turn my attention back to the brochure. "It says that before the Gibsons bought the place, this used to be a blacksmith shop."

"Oh. Well, that makes more sense," Daphne says. "It looks like whenever the blacksmith made a new branding iron or something, he tested it by branding his wall."

"Huh." I reach out to touch the shallow, blackened indentations running along the wall, and I can picture the blacksmith at work, pulling red glowing pieces of iron out of his smoking furnace, picking up a sledge hammer to pound them into the right shapes on his enormous anvil.

"Do you think there's a clue in here? Does 'Dear Lord's Prime' make any sense to you?" I ask Daphne. She and her family go to church, at least every once in a while, and I know she's taken a couple of Bible classes.

She takes the riddle from me and reads the line:

If your thoughts fall into line,
You'll recognize Our Dear Lord's prime.

Her lips make a sound like an impatient horse. "I've never heard of it, but look at all these markings on the wall. It could be almost any one of them."

Daphne's right. From one side to the other, the wall is filled with markings. They include letters of the alphabet, numbers, shapes, curlicues, and other designs that can only have been cattle brands for local ranchers.

"If there is something related to the Bible," Daphne concludes, "it'll take a religious studies expert to figure it out."

I sigh. "Or someone who lived a hundred years ago."

Ten

That night after dinner, Daphne and I sit at our campsite's picnic table. The gas-fired Coleman lantern quietly roars like a tiny jet airplane engine as we flip through Daphne's copy of the Bible. After an hour of searching, Daphne shakes her head.

"I don't see anything about God's or Jesus's prime."

I throw up my hands. "What does that even mean? Are they talking about when Jesus was his healthiest—you know, when he was in his prime of life? Or when he was spreading God's Word to everyone?"

"It might not have anything to do with Jesus. Maybe it focuses on God instead. I wish we had an Internet connection around here. We could punch in the phrase and see if anything comes up on a search."

"Well, I think I read that the vigilantes put in a high-speed connection back in the 1860s. They took it out again when the robbers started emailing each other to find out when the gold shipments were leaving town on the stagecoach."

Daphne punches me in the arm. "Very funny."

"Ow." I say, and I actually mean it this time.

Just then, Dad walks up. "Bible study?"

"Uh, no," I tell him, trying to think of some logical explanation for what we're doing. Daphne and I have debated whether or not we should share the treasure note and clues with Dad One and Dad Two. We've decided that for now, at least, we're going to keep them to ourselves. It's not that we don't trust our dads. It's just that, well, they *are* scientists. As soon as we tell them about the treasure, they're going to start asking a bunch of questions, coming up with their own theories, and taking over the whole thing. Plus, they'll probably give us all kinds of warnings about what not to do. They just can't help themselves.

Still, we do need to explain why we're sitting next to a lantern at night, looking at the Bible.

"It's our *Highlights* article," Daphne says. "We thought there might be some good quote we could use."

"Uh, yeah," I join in. "Something about dogs to spruce up the piece a little bit."

"Dogs?" Dad asks, surprised. "You think there's something about dogs in the Bible?"

"Uh..."

Daphne again steps in. "Actually, the King James Bible contains at least forty references to dogs."

My eyes snap to Daphne, and I think, *Does she really know this, or is she making it up?* Either way,

I give her credit for thinking fast.

"The problem," she continues, without skipping a tail wag, "is that every dog reference is negative. The Bible just doesn't seem to think very highly of Man's Best Friend. Still, we don't have any other books around, so we thought we might as well give the Bible a try."

Dad seems satisfied—and a little impressed. "Ah, um, well, don't stay up too late. We've got another long day tomorrow."

Which turns out to be an understatement.

The next morning, we take the OFGOV out of Bannack, but not far. Just past the "new" cemetery, Lens hangs a right, drops our vehicle into low gear, and starts grinding along a dirt and gravel road as it snakes and turns up into the sagebrush-covered hills. After a couple of miles, the road joins the original stagecoach road leading up out of Bannack toward another great Montana gold rush town, Virginia City, sixty miles to the east. Soon, we reach one of Montana's most famous landmarks, a chunk of red quartzite bigger than a house.

Len pulls over and we pile out.

"Here it is," Dad explains. "Road Agents Rock. Do you know about it already, Daphne?"

"Oh, she knows *everything* about Bannack already," I say.

"*No,*" Daphne replies, giving me a shove. "I mean

I've heard of Road Agents Rock before, but that's about it."

"Well," my dad tells her. "This is supposedly where a lot of the stagecoach hold-ups happened back in the day. The stage—loaded with gold—would come grinding up the hill from Bannack on its way to Virginia City or elsewhere. By the time the stage reached Road Agents Rock here, the horses, chests heaving, were tired and moving slow. That's when the bad guys, or 'road agents', would jump out and hold up the stage."

"You know, after they emailed each other that the stage was coming," I tell Daphne.

Daphne sticks her tongue out at me, then studies the area. After a moment, she says, "You'd think the stage drivers would get used to getting robbed here, wouldn't they? Maybe have their guns ready?"

Len and Dad both laugh. "Yeah, you'd think so."

"In *fact*," I inform everyone. "The whole Road Agents Rock thing is just a big myth. Arlis told me that there was never a single documented case of a robbery happening right here."

Everyone looks at me, surprised.

"Is that so?" Len asks.

"Yep. The book I've been reading talks about all kinds of hold-ups, too, and not one of them mentions this place."

"Too bad," Len says wistfully. "It's a good story."

That doesn't mean Road Agents Rock isn't

interesting. As we stand there, Dad explains that one big mystery—a geological mystery—is how this big chunk of quartzite ended up right here.

"This rock is at least a mile from any other quartzite outcrop," he explains. "Was it carried on a landslide? Did a big flood wash it over here? I just don't know."

With that little bit of trivia tickling our brains, Daphne and I start exploring around the rock. We can still see the deep ruts that hundreds of stage-coaches and wagons carved into the soil as they passed by. The ground is also littered with old, rusted cans that used to contain food.

"Apparently," Dad tells us all, "this used to be a popular picnic spot for the people in Bannack."

We spend fifteen minutes walking all around the large landmark, studying it. Daphne and I look for old names scratched into the rock. We think we can make out a random letter here or there, but weather and orange, green, and black lichens have obliterated any meaningful graffiti.

We're stooping down to try to read some of the labels on the rusted old cans, when Dad pulls out a topographical map. "Slate, Daphne, over here."

We join him, and I'm thinking he and Len plan to show us where we're all going to be working. Instead, he surprises us.

"We're going to split up today," he says. "We'll leave the Travelall here, and Len and I are going to examine some of these old mine sites."

He points to some locations on the map that have little crossed pick axes on them to indicate mines.

"We want you and Daphne to take this map and a GPS, and collect some rock samples over in this section here," he says, pointing to another area about a mile up the road.

Daphne and I glance at each other, eyebrows raised. The dads have never trusted us with an assignment quite this big before.

"Include mine sites and test holes," Len elaborates. "Wherever you find some interesting looking rock samples, take a GPS reading."

"Make sure you keep track of which rock samples belong to which site," Dad says—as if I haven't been doing that for the past two weeks. Still, I have to work to keep the grin off my face.

"Do you want us to look for gossan, too?" Daphne asks.

Show off, I think, but Dad says, "Sure. But it might be hard to find. The area's probably pretty overgrown."

Len pulls out a pair of matched two-way radios from the OFGOV, and hands one of them to me. "Take this. It should have a range of a couple of miles. We want you to stay together and check in with us frequently. Here's an extra pair of batteries in case yours run out."

"And don't go into any old mines you come across,

either," Dad warns us. "Just collect samples from the mine dumps—the extra rock they pulled out of the tunnels."

"Dad, I know what a mine dump is," I say.

"Hey, how come *Slate* gets to carry the radio?" Daphne complains.

Len looks at her with a face remarkably similar to Daphne's own 'irritated amphibian' expression. "Daphne, I am sure Slate will let you carry the radio sometimes."

"Fat chance," I mutter under my breath.

"Here," my dad tells her, handing her another electronic device. "You can carry the GPS."

Daphne smirks at me. "Let's go."

Eleven

We hike up the dirt-and-gravel road for maybe a mile, stopping every few minutes to check our GPS location. You probably already know that GPS stands for Gold Prospecting System. Just kidding. It actually stands for Global Positioning System. It uses satellites to beam your exact location to you, and is especially useful for field scientists doing research—and for tourists desperate to locate a restroom before their kids have an accident all over the fuzzy seats of their brand new minivans. Anyway, when we reach the edge of section 27 on our map, Daphne takes a compass bearing, and we both start walking east, across a rising slope of sagebrush.

"I can't believe the dads are letting us do this," Daphne gushes.

"Well, they should. I mean, how many times have we assisted them in the field?"

"I know. I know. But still..."

I can't help smiling proudly, myself.

We have no trouble finding interesting rock outcrops on the open hillside we're hiking on. We head to the first one—a red chunk of rock jutting up out of the sagebrush—and Daphne gives me the

GPS coordinates. I write them down in a yellow waterproof notebook, and then we both pick out some good-looking rock samples. Ore samples don't look all shiny and golden like you might expect. They're often rusty-looking and you have to break them open to see if the quartz inside might have any gold particles in it. Dad One and Dad Two do that. Daphne and I just put the rocks in zip-lock bags, label them with an indelible marker, and toss them in my pack.

"Ugh," I moan, feeling the added weight as I re-hoist my pack. "You're carrying the next batch of rock samples."

"Don't be such a *boy*," Daphne tells me.

I stick my tongue out at her, and we both laugh.

As we walk, we occasionally kick over some soil or pull up some grass to get a look at what's underneath.

"Here's some gossan," I tell Daphne.

She stops.

I reach down and pick up a chunk of yellowish-orange rock.

"That's gossan, all right," Daphne confirms.

Gossan, also called *iron cap*, is weathered rock that sits at the top of a vein or layer of ore. What happens is that over millions of years, rain washes out a lot of the metals in the gossan. The metals sink down through the rock until they hit the water table and come out of solution, where they can build up into extremely rich deposits. Gossan often told old-time prospectors "Dig here!" If the miner could blast down through the gossan until he reached the layer of rock where the metals had accumulated, he might discover a rich deposit of gold, silver, copper, or other minerals. In fact, from where we're standing now, we can see at least three or four "test holes" that miners have dug over the last 150 years.

Daphne again reads the GPS and tells me the latitude and longitude coordinates of our location, and I mark them on the map. Then, we continue walking east.

Suddenly, Len's voice crackles over our two-way radio.

"Slate, Daphne, come in."

I pull the radio from my pocket and press the "talk" button. "Roger," I say, "this is Fire Team One. We have successfully parachuted behind enemy lines and are about to blow-up enemy headquarters."

Daphne rolls her eyes, but I can hear Len chuckle on the other end.

"Glad everything's going okay. You find anything yet?"

"Yep," I tell him. "And we have launched full-scale mining operations and are making so much money, you will not—I repeat—will NOT have to pay for our college educations."

"Give me that!" Daphne tries to grab the radio

from me, but I deftly swing away from her.

"Well, that's a relief," Len's voice tells us. "Check in the next time you find something."

"Roger that. Fire Team One, over and out."

As I return the radio to my pocket, Daphne says, "You are so annoying sometimes."

I grin, and we continue walking up the slope.

Soon, our path leads us right to a full-blown mine. It consists of two tunnels—a horizontal tunnel that probably follows a vein of rock that contains the gold or silver, and a vertical shaft farther up the hill that helps ventilate the mine. Both tunnels are partially caved-in, but we can still see the rough wooden beams the miners used to keep the horizontal tunnel from collapsing. Littered all around the area are rusting tin cans, old-fashioned square nails, and other artifacts. It doesn't take a detective to tell that the mine is very, very old.

"Wow," Daphne says. "Can you imagine digging this all out by hand?"

"Well, they probably used dynamite, too."

"You know what I mean. Either way, it was a lot of work. I wonder if it paid off for them?"

I consider the dry hills around us. One of the problems with a lot of mining areas, my dad has explained to me, is that they weren't close to water. The miners needed water to separate the metals from the ore. At a dry site like this, they would have had to cart all the raw ore by horse and wagon back into Bannack and Grasshopper Creek for processing.

"It wouldn't have been worth it unless this was a very rich site," I say.

That, of course, is why modern mining companies look over old mining areas again. Ore that wouldn't have been worth mining 150 years ago using primitive methods can reap rich profits with modern mining techniques.

Once again, we mark our location and collect a couple of rock samples—which I place in *Daphne's* pack. We are just about to continue our search when a gruff voice behind us shouts, "Hey! What are you doing here?"

Daphne and I spin around to see a slender, red-faced man marching up to us. The man looks like he's maybe thirty or thirty-five years old. He is wearing brown Carhartt pants and a long-sleeved shirt. Dirty blonde hair sticks out from under an auto parts store cap. This is public land, and my first impression is that he's a local rancher out grazing his herd nearby. Whoever he is, he is not pleased to run into us.

"What are you kids doing here?" he repeats.

"We're helping our fathers," Daphne tells him. "Looking at the rocks in the area."

That stops the man, and I can almost hear his brain clicking over. "Well," he stammers, still almost shouting. "Don't you know this place is dangerous? There's mines like this one everywhere. You might not even know you're on top of one and BOOM, it could collapse right under you. Swallow you whole!"

For once, even Daphne can't figure out what to say. I'm sure her heart is pounding, just like mine is. Even in my fright, though, I am sensing something else going on. I can't quite put my finger on it, but something's not right about this guy.

"You kids need to get out of here," he tells us. "Tell your parents not to let their kids play in such a dangerous area."

Now, I'm getting a bit steamed myself. "We weren't *playing!*"

"And we're not *kids!*" Daphne tells him.

The man takes a step closer to us. "*Whatever* you were doing and *whoever* you are, you need to get out of here."

The man doesn't say "or else", but his threat is loud and clear.

I quickly debate standing my ground, but my Inner Coward gives me better advice. Daphne and I quickly turn around and high-tail it back down the hill.

Twelve

We don't say a word until we reach the dirt road that leads back toward Road Agents Rock. Then, Daphne says, "That man had no right to tell us to leave."

"Who does he think he is, anyway?" I agree. "This is public land."

"And we know more about mining than he ever will."

"That's right. What should we do about it?"

Daphne kicks at a rock in the road. "I know what I'd like to do. I'd like to shove him down one of those ventilation shafts!"

I have to admit that I love seeing Daphne erupt—especially when it's not directed at me. One of the things I like most about her is that she goes ballistic every once in a while. But as we walk, I am also still thinking about the man we encountered, and feeling that something about the guy just wasn't right.

Using the two-way radio, we locate our fathers, who happen to be examining another mine site close to Road Agents Rock. On the radio, I don't tell them why we are returning early, but they look a little concerned when we arrive.

"Everything all right?" Dad asks.

"You didn't finish already, did you?" Len says.

We explain to them what happened. When we finish, Dad looks at Len. "What do you think?"

Len turns to me. "You said he might be a rancher?"

"Well, he was dressed in Carhartts," I say, referring to the brand of rugged clothing favored by a lot of ranchers and farmers in the West. "But the Carhartts were brand new, which seemed peculiar."

"I noticed his hands and neck were pale," Daphne adds. "I've never seen a rancher with pale skin before."

Len turns back to my dad. "Well, maybe we should head back into Dillon tomorrow, to the BLM office. Find out who holds the grazing leases around here, and contact them directly."

Dad exhales, frustrated. "Probably a smart idea. I hate to lose another field day driving into town, though."

"Well, why don't I take Slate and Daphne with me, and you can work out here?"

Dad nods. "If you don't mind, Len, that would be great. All right with you two?"

"Sure," Daphne and I say at the same time. "We want to go to the library anyway, and look up some stuff on the Internet."

"Good, then it's settled," Len says.

I don't even hear Dad leave the tent the next

morning. Len lets me sleep in, and when I finally emerge, yawning, I find him looking over some maps at the picnic table.

"Where's Daphne?" I ask.

"Oh, she got up to take some sunrise photos in Bannack. Want some coffee?"

I scrunch up my face, and Len laughs. "It's pretty awful stuff, isn't it?"

"You can say that again."

"It's pretty awful stuff, isn't it?"

I groan. "Not you, too."

"Sorry," Len says, then adds, "I thought we'd head out as soon as Daphne gets back. Sound good?"

I nod, and make myself some instant oatmeal with raisins. As I'm washing my bowl, Daphne comes hurrying back into camp. She rushes over to me, bouncing up and down like she's got grasshoppers in her boots.

"What is it?" I grumble, still not fully awake.

Daphne gestures to Len, and then motions me over toward the creek. When we're out of earshot, she says, "Slate, I figured it out!"

"Huh?"

"The clue. I figured out Dear Lord's Prime!"

That wakes me up. "You *did*?"

"Yes! I walked to the other end of Bannack to see if I could get some good morning light off the old buildings. I was walking back and stopped to take some pictures of some rabbits grazing nearby.

They ran away when I—"

"Will you get to the point?"

"Uh—yeah! Look!"

She turns on her camera and quickly flicks through several images on the LED screen. Then, she hands it to me.

I adjust the angle of the camera so I can view the image better, and see a close-up of some of the brands that were burned into the wall of the Gibson house. The one that stands out is the number '7'.

I am still not getting it, and Daphne reads the dull look in my eyes.

She explains. "*Prime* doesn't refer to how healthy or active Jesus was. It refers to prime *numbers*. A prime number is a number that is only divisible by itself and the number one, and—"

"I *know* what a prime number is," I interrupt her, even though I know she's probably just trying to get my goat.

"So you see," she says with a grin, "'7' is the only prime number burned into that wall."

"But what does 7 have to do with God or Jesus?" I ask, still not making the connection.

"Probably nothing, but look at the brand next to it."

Right next to the '7', I see a circle with the letters 'JC' branded into it.

Finally, the light clicks on. "Okay, okay. JC— Jesus Christ."

Daphne slaps me on the back. "There's hope for you yet, Slate."

"Come on, let's go!" Len calls from the OFGOV.

Daphne turns off her camera. "Coming!"

Thirteen

On the drive into Dillon, we pass both sheriff's and highway patrol cruisers.

"That's odd," Len observes. "I wonder what's going on?"

"Maybe the governor's dog ran away again?" I suggest.

Daphne snorts, and Len says, "Let's hope not."

Once we get into town, he drops us at the public library. "After I go to the BLM office, I've got some other things to do," he says. "How long do you need?"

Daphne and I trade looks. "A couple of hours?" she suggests.

"Okay, why don't we meet at the bookstore just up the street about noon. Then, we can grab some lunch before heading back to Bannack."

The OFGOV rumbles up South Idaho Street and we enter the library. Since Daphne has apparently solved the next riddle in our quest for the vigilantes' treasure, we actually no longer have an urgent reason to get on the Internet. Daphne, though, wants to check her email, so I follow her toward the computer terminals. As we walk past the library newspaper rack, I suddenly grasp Daphne's arm.

"Look."

I pick up the morning edition of the *Dillon Tribune*. The headline shouts,

ART HEIST MANHUNT CONTINUES

Daphne and I take the paper to a nearby table and scoot together in adjacent chairs. Our faces almost touching, we begin silently reading the story.

Daphne's closeness is more than a little distracting. Every time she exhales, her warm breath washes over my skin, and I again start wondering how her lips would feel against mine. If we weren't in the library…well, I'd probably chicken out again.

Pay attention, I tell myself, forcing my mind back to the article. I keep reading, and the third paragraph especially catches my eye:

> *Law officers initially thought that the thief managed to flee Beaverhead County. However, eyewitness reports indicate that the suspect most likely is still in the area.*
>
> *"It looks like our roadblocks successfully prevented the suspect from leaving the county,"* Dillon Police Chief Bertek *told the* Dillon Tribune. *"We do not know where he is, but hope to find him soon."*

"Well, that explains the law enforcement cruisers we saw on the way in," I tell Daphne.

"Shush!"

I glance over to see that her eyes are already devouring the article's last few lines.

After finishing, she stabs the last paragraph with her finger. "Look at this," she says. "The Russell paintings he stole were on loan. One was from the Montana Historical Society in Helena, the other from the C.M. Russell Museum in Great Falls. Together, the paintings are worth an estimated four million dollars."

"Four million?" I say, reading the last paragraph for myself. "I knew Russell's art was worth a lot, but not that much."

"Have you ever heard of these paintings?"

Daphne is asking me because my mom is a painter, and she's taught me a lot about different artists over the years. Russell happens to be one of my favorites.

I read the titles out loud. *"Bronc to Breakfast* and *The Fireboat.* I may have heard of the second one, but Russell made like 4,000 works of art in his lifetime. Let's look 'em up."

We move to an unoccupied computer terminal, and Daphne punches in the first painting's name.

"Nice," she says, as an image of the painting pops up. It shows a fiery horse bucking through a camp cooking fire, a rider trying desperately to control him as the cook and other cowboys watch or scramble out of the way.

"Look at that!" I laugh, pointing to a frying pan full of unidentified breakfast food being launched into mid-air.

Daphne snorts appreciatively, then calls up the second painting. It has a more serious tone, depicting a group of mounted Indians at dusk, perched on a high bluff. Like many of Russell's paintings, the light on the Indians' faces has spectacular orange and yellow hues, but it's what they're looking at that gives weight to the painting. Far below, a lone steamboat is pushing its way up the Missouri River. One of the Indians rests his chin in his hands in thought while the central Indian is saying something in sign language to one of his companions.

"I wonder what he's saying?" Daphne muses.

"Probably not too hard to guess," I answer.

Daphne nods. "I guess the steamboat and setting sun represent the beginning of the end for the Indian tribes' freedom, huh?"

"Yeah," I mumble, lost in the painting.

We stare at the image for another few seconds. Then, Daphne asks, "Have you ever heard of Russell paintings getting stolen before?"

I shake my head.

She types in some new searches. Soon, she comes up with a website called "Art Thefts". Daphne locates an index by artist and clicks on 'R' for Russell. Neither of us is prepared for what pops up.

Daphne's hazel eyes bore into mine. "Can you believe this?"

Listed on the computer screen are more than a dozen thefts of Russell paintings, sketches, and sculptures that have occurred in the last three years. Many of the stolen pieces are valued in excess of one million dollars. One lists at almost five million!

"Seems like someone really wants Russell's art," Daphne says.

"Well, we don't really know if that's an unusual number. Click on some other artists."

Daphne looks up some other famous and not-so-famous artists. All of them except Van Gogh and Picasso have fewer—far fewer—cases in the last three years. "Do you think these Russell robberies were all committed by the same person?"

The website indicates that the Russells have been stolen all over the country, mostly from smaller museums and private homes.

"I have no idea," I reply. "But, these paintings are part of Montana's heritage. Shoot, the whole world's heritage! I sure hope they find whoever's behind it."

We leave the library and head up to The Bookstore—and that really is its name. It's a good one, too—the store, that is. They've got an especially great section of young adult books that you wouldn't normally find in a small-town shop. I scan the racks for graphic novels while Daphne looks through the fantasy section. Fortunately, she has finished the *Vampires in Hollyweird* series, but the new book she picks out doesn't look much better.

"Have you read this?" she asks, holding up a paperback called *Werewundrels*. The book has a picture of a savage—yet oddly handsome—creature embracing a beautiful, serious-looking young woman.

You have got to be kidding! I think to myself. *Who came up with that stupid idea?* With Daphne, however, I've learned to bite my tongue when it comes to giving opinions on books.

"I've heard it's good," she says.

I can't tell if she's serious, or is just trying to get a reaction from me, so I take the safe approach and answer, "Uh-huh."

Fortunately, before I have to say anything else, Len walks into the store.

Fourteen

After chatting with The Bookstore's owner, Debbie, Len asks us, "So, where do you want to have lunch?"

"Sparky's!" we both shout.

Len rolls his eyes good-naturedly, and we start walking toward the OFGOV.

"Hey, what did you find out about that man who yelled at us yesterday?" Daphne asks him. "Was he a rancher?"

"That's the funny thing," Len says as we turn a corner onto East Bannack Street. Two blocks ahead of us stands the handsome Beaverhead County Courthouse, and right on cue, the courthouse bells start ringing in the lunchtime hour.

"What's a funny thing?" I ask Len, raising my voice.

"Well, the BLM guy said nobody is grazing that area right now."

"Could it have been a small-time miner?"

"I asked about that, too. But the BLM ranger was quite familiar with the area and felt certain there aren't any active claims in that section."

We reach the OFGOV as the last vibrations of the bells die out, and we all climb in. Len puts his key in the ignition and starts up the engine.

Before he can put it into 'Drive', however, Daphne asks, "Well, who do you think the guy was?"

As soon as she says it, our heads whip around to look at each other.

"Could he be...?" I exclaim.

"Do you think...?" Daphne asks.

Len swings around in the driver's seat to look at us. "Who? Could he be who?"

"Well," I tell him. "The newspaper article we read at the library said that the thief is still at large."

Len looks confused. "What thief? You mean the man who broke into the art museum a couple of days ago?"

"*Yes.*" Daphne's eyes blaze with excitement. "The police think he's hiding out right here in Beaverhead County!"

I chime in. "Plus, the man we saw kind of matches the description the police chief gave out before!"

"I thought the robber had a mask on," Len says.

"He did, but I mean his physical description. Medium-build, that sort of thing."

"Why would he be wearing Carhartt pants, though?" Daphne muses.

"*New* Carhartts," I point out. "Maybe he's trying to blend in. You said yourself that he didn't look much like a rancher, even under the clothes."

Daphne nods.

Len says. "Well, if you kids are serious, we

probably ought to report this."

Daphne excitedly sucks in her breath and looks at me. "It really could be him."

"I agree."

Len turns the motor back off and pulls the key out. "Okay," he says. "The Dillon Police Station is right up the street. Let's walk."

We climb back out of the OFGOV and cover another couple of blocks to the courthouse. The station is actually a combined police and sheriff's office, and it's attached to the north side of the courthouse. For such a small town, the station is buzzing. Uniformed officers and "civilians" are standing around having conversations. Through open doors, I also notice Chief Bertek in a conference room off to the side, and a camera crew packing up next to him. *They must have just conducted an interview,* I tell myself.

We march up to a glass window with a speaker system embedded in it. A uniformed woman wearing a silver shield and her hair pulled back tight asks, "Yes? What can I help you with?"

Daphne is better at these situations than I am, so I let her do the talking. In a bold voice, she says, "We think we may have seen the suspect in the art theft case."

The entire room hushes and I glance around to see all eyes on Daphne. The camera crew hurries to break out its gear again.

I don't think we could have surprised the desk

sergeant more if we'd announced that we were the long-lost children she'd given up for adoption. She tasers us with her eyes and says, "You mean the person who robbed the art museum?"

Daphne nods. "That's right."

"Okay," she says, standing up. "Perhaps we should move into the conference room."

Before we can escape, a reporter jams a microphone into Daphne's face.

"Little girl," the reporter says.

I laugh.

Daphne shoots me a scowl and tells the reporter, "I am *not* a little girl."

"Oh, uh," the reporter fumbles.

But then Daphne decides to cut him some slack. "Did you have a question?" she asks in a fake syrupy voice.

"W-well," the reporter stammers. Not only is the guy lousy with kids, he's not even sure what to ask. "I-I was just wondering if you could tell us about the man you saw."

"I didn't say he was a man," Daphne tells him. "You are making a premature inference."

"He was a *she*?"

Len and I both laugh this time.

By now, the desk sergeant has come out of her glass-enclosed cubicle. "All right, all right," she tells the reporter. "That's enough. We'll let you know if there's any new information."

The officer herds Daphne, Len, and me into the room next to the reception area. The room has a long table in it, and several other people, including Chief Bertek, crowd in after us before someone closes the door. Besides the police uniforms, I see sheriff's and highway patrol uniforms, too. One guy stands a little apart from everyone else. He's wearing a dark suit, tie, and sunglasses.

"Have a seat." The woman motions us to some chairs, but everyone else remains standing.

"So," Chief Bertek tells us, "why do you think you saw the suspect?"

Taking turns talking, Daphne and I describe our experience with "Mr. Carhartt" the day before. The Chief stops us every once in a while to clarify a point or ask a question, but mostly he lets us talk.

"So, that's all we know," Daphne tells them when we're finished.

Chief Bertek looks up at the man in the black suit. "What do you think?"

The man dips his head slightly to the side. "Could be our man."

"Could you take us to the place you saw this guy?" the Chief asks us.

I ask, "Can we get some lunch first?"

Fifteen

Daphne and I ride in the back seat of an unmarked black SUV, with a sheriff's deputy driving and the man in the dark suit and sunglasses riding shotgun. Len follows behind with a Dillon police officer in the OFGOV. After a quick stop at the McDonald's drive-thru, we head back toward Bannack.

The man in the dark suit takes a sip of his Diet Coke and turns around. "We haven't met yet, but I'm Agent Bullock."

I shove some French fries into my mouth and shake his hand. "You mean agent, as in FBI agent?"

"Yes," he answers stiffly. "Federal Bureau of Investigation."

Duh, I think to myself.

Daphne swallows a bite of fish sandwich. "Are you here because this is tied to the other Russell art thefts?"

We can't see Agent Bullock's eyes behind his dark sunglasses, but the pause in his voice betrays surprise. "How do you know about those?"

"We looked them up online this morning," Daphne explains with a certain flirty tone she reserves for handsome men. I scowl and reassert control over the conversation.

"It looks to us like someone is trying to build a Charlie Russell collection without paying for it," I say.

Agent Bullock's mouth finally softens into a trace of a smile. "Hm. Maybe you should come work for the Bureau."

"I would *love* that," Daphne gushes.

I give her my disapproving glare, but she ignores it. "So do you think the guy who is doing the robberies is actually the one keeping the paintings?" she asks.

"I'm not at liberty to discuss too much about the case," Bullock answers, "but we don't think so. We believe that the actual thief—or thieves—are being hired by someone else. Someone with money."

"But not enough money to buy the paintings legally," I say.

"Again, we don't know. Many of Russell's finest paintings never come up for sale. They are locked away in museums and private collections. It could be that this is the only way that person can build the collection he or she wants."

I unwrap my cheeseburger and take a huge bite, then wash it down with some chocolate milkshake.

"We noticed that most of the thefts are from private homes or smaller museums," Daphne says. "Is that because there's less security to deal with in those kinds of places?"

"Very perceptive," Bullock answers.

Daphne beams.

"Two years ago," Bullock continues, "there was an attempted burglary at the Gilcrease Museum in Tulsa, Oklahoma. The Gilcrease has one of the best Russell collections in the world, and the thief actually removed a very famous Russell masterpiece off of the wall before tripping an alarm system and fleeing. After that, the thieves have targeted smaller venues."

"You think the guy who broke into the Gilcrease Museum was the same guy as the one who broke into the UM Western museum?"

"Again, we're not sure."

"Haven't you collected any DNA evidence?" I ask this question both because I'm curious, and because I'd like to make Agent Bullock look bad in front of Daphne.

Bullock purses his lips. "Again, I'm not at liberty to say."

I smirk, and think, *You mean you've botched the case until now.*

We slip into silence while we eat the rest of our meals. By the time we've finished, we've driven over Badger Pass and turned off Highway 278, onto the access road to Bannack.

After a mile or so, Daphne instructs the driver, "Turn left up here, on the road in front of that cemetery."

With Len following behind, we turn and grind

up the dirt road past Road Agents Rock. When we reach the place where Daphne and I were working yesterday, I say, "Stop here."

The mine is about a half-mile from the road and we lead Bullock, the officers, and Len up the slope through the sage and rabbit bush. Daphne and I set a fast pace, and I note with satisfaction that Bullock's patent leather shoes are quickly coated in white powdery dirt—the thin layer of calcium carbonate, or *caliche*, that covers the area.

By the time we reach the mine, the 6500-foot elevation has Agent Bullock gasping like a mule. He doesn't admit it.

"Is that..." he says, gulping air. "Is that mine... safe...to go into?"

Len peers into the horizontal tunnel. "No guarantees, but if only one person enters at a time and moves carefully, it ought to be okay. Just take care not to bump any of those support beams."

Agent Bullock hesitates. Then, the sheriff's deputy bends over and says, "Looks like fresh tracks going into the mine." He straightens up and looks at Agent Bullock. "I don't mind goin' in. I've been in a few mines before."

Bullock pulls back his shoulder blades and says, "I'll do it. I don't want any contamination of the crime scene."

After that insulting comment, the sheriff's deputy and police officer look like they'd like to contaminate the crime scene with Agent Bullock's rear end.

But the sheriff's deputy says, "Well in that case, we'll just look around out here where it's nice and safe."

I stifle a laugh, but Agent Bullock misses the sarcasm and heads into the mine.

While he's doing that, Daphne, Len, and I fan out with the deputy and police officer, scouring the surrounding area. After about ten minutes, I hear Agent Bullock calling us back. I am just about to return when my eye catches something small and brightly-colored tangled up in some sagebrush branches.

Litter.

Anger rises up inside of me. I swear I just don't get people who throw their trash everywhere. Most Montanans would never dream of throwing their garbage out in a beautiful place like this. Unfortunately, there are still a few litterbugs who treat the outdoors as their personal garbage dump. They don't think twice about tossing cigarette butts out car windows or dropping soda bottles and candy wrappers anywhere.

"Idiot," I mutter. I lean down and pull the plastic—a wrapper from a watermelon-flavored Jolly Rancher candy—out of the sage bush and shove it into my pocket. Then, I make my way back to join the others.

"Did you find anything?" the deputy asks the

FBI guy. Agent Bullock finally takes off his jacket to reveal wet stains under his armpits.

"Nothing much. Someone has obviously been here, but the place is cleaned out."

"Maybe he got spooked when he ran into Slate and Daphne," Len suggests.

The three lawmen nod.

"You guys find anything?" Agent Bullock asks.

"Just footprints," the police officer says.

"The same," adds the deputy. "Look like about a size 10."

"We'll want to make some latex impressions of those," Bullock says. "Otherwise, I don't think we have much to go on."

"Wouldn't hurt to do some checking around the area," the deputy sheriff says. "Drive around, maybe talk to some residents down near Bannack to see if they've seen anything."

Bullock nods. "I agree—just to make sure."

Sixteen

"**H**ey, what's going on around here?" Dusty and tired after a day of hiking the hills, my dad shuffles into camp, where Daphne and I are playing the tie-breaker in a five-game match of cribbage. I am leading this game by about ten holes and am hoping to "skunk" her. Daphne, though, has just laid down a good hand.

"Fifteen-two, fifteen-four, fifteen-six, and a double straight are fourteen," Daphne counts out triumphantly. She advances her peg around the corner onto fourth street.

So much for my skunk.

Then, looking entirely too smug—not to mention cute—Daphne says, "And now let's see what's in my crib?"

She flips over the four down-facing cards in her crib—the extra hand that belongs to the dealer. When she sees the cards, she pumps her fist in the air. "YES!"

I moan. Her three fives and Jack of hearts impale my spirit like a pick axe. "You are *soooo* lucky."

"Not luck, Slate Stephens. Skill."

I frown as she counts up a phenomenal score, which not only vaults her past me, but wins the game.

She beams. "Twenty-three! Set, game, match!"

"Cheater," I grumble, but I know when I've been whooped fair and square.

"So," my dad tries again, lowering his pack to the ground. "What's with all the sheriff and police cars everywhere?"

Dad scoots onto the picnic bench next to me and listens while Len, Daphne, and I recount the morning's events. When we're through, Dad whistles and says, "So the Wild West returns to Bannack, huh?"

"Yep," I tell him. "The Vigilance Committee requests your presence at their meeting at the Masonic Lodge tonight. Bring some rope."

Dad and Len chuckle.

"So what have they found out?" Dad asks in a more serious tone. "Has anyone stopped by to give you an update?"

"A sheriff's deputy came over about an hour ago," Daphne tells him. "She said they haven't found anything, and that most likely, the guy we saw had nothing to do with the art museum robbery."

"Who was he then?"

"They think maybe he was poaching deer," I say. "With so many people out of work these days, the deputy said they're seeing a lot more illegal hunting for food."

"I'm glad he wasn't armed when you two ran into him."

Len shakes his head and sighs. "Me too. You'd

both better stay close to us from now on."

I ask, "Is it okay if Daphne and I just walk into Bannack. We wanted to work on our—"

"We like looking around there," Daphne cuts me off.

"Oh, uh, yeah," I say.

Dad raises his eyebrows. "You wanted to work on your *what?*"

"Uh…"

"Our photography," Daphne steps in. "Bannack's the perfect place for it."

Usually, the dads would just let us go, but Len says, "I don't think that's a good idea until we have a better picture of what's going on around here."

"I agree," Dad says. "You two stick around camp until we ascertain that that guy wasn't the robber—and that the man you did see isn't dangerous. Besides Slate, after I get cleaned up, I need to redeem your honor by beating Daphne at cribbage."

Daphne snorts derisively. "You wish."

The next morning, Cal the campground manager swings by our campsite while we're finishing breakfast.

"Get you a cup of coffee?" Dad asks him.

Cal—who really is from California and wears a shirt blooming with hibiscus flowers to prove it—waves a hand. "Thanks. I'm all topped off. Just wanted to let you folks know that I heard from the

Beaverhead County Sheriff today that their search came up empty. They did find a rental car abandoned along a dirt road about fifteen miles from here. No sign of the guy there or here, though, so it looks like you're safe to go about your business."

"Thanks. Appreciate it," Len tells him.

Cal starts to walk back to his trailer when he stops and turns. "Oh, and thought you might like to know, there's a big storm front moving in this evening. It's gonna get pretty wet around here. Don't know if that makes much of an impact on you science guys, but it's not going to be great camping weather."

After Cal leaves, Len turns to my dad and asks, "Well, what do you want to do, Andrew?"

Dad purses his lips and scratches the two-week salt-and-pepper stubble sprouting across his cheeks. He bends over a topographical map and points to a spot just north of Road Agents Rock. "If the weather's going to close in, I'd like to get this area surveyed along here. If more than a few millimeters of rain fall, the ground around here is going to turn into gumbo, making this a tough slog later."

'Gumbo' is a term we're all way too familiar with. It's a heavy, wet mud that forms in many parts of Montana whenever it rains. It's a combination of dirt, gravel, rock, and old volcanic ash, and when it gets wet, it turns into the worst sticky mess you can imagine. It builds up on the bottoms of your boots and tries to suck you down with every step. Imagine walking around in wet concrete for an hour or so. Gumbo is worse.

Len nods at my dad's plan. "What about camp? You want to ride it out?"

My dad straightens up. "Oh, hadn't thought of that." He pauses and looks at me and Daphne. "Maybe it'd be a good chance to grab a couple of motel rooms, get cleaned up—unless you kids just want to stay camping out here in the cold, miserable rain, hail, and lightning?"

Daphne and I both break into huge grins. "Yeah! I mean, no!" I say.

"Motel rooms!" Daphne clarifies.

"Okay," Dad says. "But if we're going to do this, you and Daphne have to get our camp packed up."

"No problem," Daphne says.

"If we finish early, can we go into Bannack?" I ask.

"Yeah," Dad says, "But be back here by three p.m. at the latest. You still got your two-way radio?"

I pat my pocket. "Right here."

"Good. I don't know if the signal will reach us from down in this canyon, but keep it on you just in case."

Seventeen

Daphne and I pack up camp in Olympic gold medal time. Daphne stows all of her and Len's stuff while I do the same for Dad and me. Then, we work together to take down the tents and load them into the OFGOV. We finish by 10 a.m., so we grab our daypacks and start walking toward Bannack.

It is a beautiful day. The cottonwood trees along Grasshopper Creek shimmer in the full morning light. The warm sun feels delicious on my face and there's no sign of the approaching storm in the sky.

I unfold the sheet of clues while we walk. "So," I say, "Where are we?"

Daphne seizes the piece of paper and studies it. "Well, we've got Our Dear Lord's prime number—7," she reminds me.

"Oh, yeah. And since you're so *grabby* this morning, why don't you read the whole riddle over again?"

She reads:

From the place of Plummer's demise,
Walk to town to seek your prize.

A yellow journal points you to
The location of your second clue.

If your thoughts fall into line,
You'll recognize Our Dear Lord's prime.

To a House Divided, take this mark,
And count to how a wolf is cloaked.

And with that precious knowledge stored,
Find the dwelling of one once adored.

"So," I say. "We're looking for a 'house divided', right?"

"Do you remember reading anything about that in your book?"

"No," I tell Daphne, plucking a stem of sagebrush as I walk. "Unless…"

"Unless what?"

I crush the sagebrush leaves between my fingers and lift them to my nose. The pungent fragrance of mint shooting up my nasal passages makes me wince.

"Hello? Slate?"

I shake off a sneeze. "Well, I'm not sure this is it, but Bannack and all the vigilante stuff started during the Civil War."

"Ah," Daphne nods. "And didn't Lincoln mention something about a 'House Divided' in one of his famous speeches?"

"That sounds right." I hold the piece of sage to

Daphne's nose, and her head snaps back a couple of inches.

"Whew! That's strong."

"Anyway," I continue, "one thing I read is that here in Bannack, the Union sympathizers usually lived on one side of Grasshopper Creek in the area called Yankee Flats. Confederate sympathizers lived on the other side of the creek—the north side."

Daphne gives her little snort. "That's ironic—the Southerners living on the north side."

"Yeah. But all of this doesn't really help us with the clue. I mean, 'House Divided' couldn't be talking about all of Bannack, could it? How does that help us?"

Before Daphne can respond, we reach the parking lot and notice a small crowd outside of the visitor's center up ahead.

"What's going on?" Daphne asks.

"Probably a tour. Is it Saturday today?" When I'm working out in the field with my dad, I often lose track of the days.

"Yep," Daphne answers.

"Oh, well I think they have a tour every Saturday morning. It's the only time during the week when they take people into the Masonic Lodge above the school room."

"Have you been on the tour before?"

I shake my head.

"Well, let's join in. Maybe it will give us some ideas."

Arlis is leading the tour, and we fall in behind twenty or so other visitors as she starts taking us down Main Street.

"The first stop on our tour this morning is the site of the first Governor's Mansion," Arlis shouts, leading us across the street from the visitor's center. "When Sidney Edgerton brought his family to Bannack in 1863, he was not yet Governor of Montana. Montana, in fact, was still part of Idaho Territory and Edgerton was the Chief Justice—the main law man for the territory. As you can guess by the vigilante movement, he wasn't very good at his job."

Several people in the crowd chuckle.

"When Edgerton first arrived, he bought a one-room log cabin on this site for $400."

"You mean this isn't the actual Governor's house?" someone asks.

We all look at the dismal, tilting rough-hewn house I'd shown Daphne on her first day in Bannack.

"No," Arlis explains, "The original house burned in the early 1900s, and people used some of the original logs to erect this sad little building to replace it."

Daphne elbows me and whispers in an accusing voice, "You told me that was the Governor's *Mansion.* That's the last time I believe anything you tell me."

I grunt.

Then, Arlis asks, "By the way, anyone know who

Sidney Edgerton bought his house from originally?"

I raise my hand. "Henry Plummer."

Arlis smiles. "That's right—the very sheriff the vigilantes would hang just a few months later."

"Show off," Daphne whispers.

"And now," Arlis says, "if you'll follow me, we'll head down the street."

Arlis continues leading us along Main Street, stopping to talk about one building after another. I am surprised how much I learn from the tour. Arlis sprinkles in all kinds of cool little stories that aren't in the official brochure or the vigilante book that I'm reading. Halfway down the street, she halts at the Masonic Lodge and schoolhouse. We all crowd into the schoolroom where Daphne and I first found the treasure clues.

Arlis explains how the Masons built the school in 1874 for a total cost of $1500 and how it was the first public school in Montana.

"The school was used all the way up until the 1950s," Arlis says, "when there were no longer enough students to justify keeping it open. But that doesn't mean the occasional ghost doesn't return to class."

Daphne and I look at each other, and the rest of the crowd stirs.

"Life in Bannack was tough," Arlis elaborates. "Many students died of diseases such as diphtheria and smallpox and tuberculosis."

Then, Arlis does about the creepiest thing imaginable. She steps over to one of the desks, lays her hand on it, and says, "And this desk here was—or I should say *is*—inhabited by Bannack's most famous ghost, a girl named Dorothy."

Eighteen

"**S**late," Daphne hisses, "that's the desk where you found the treasure clues!"

"I know!"

"Dorothy was a beautiful fifteen year-old girl," Arlis recounts. "One day, she went swimming in Grasshopper Creek just west of here. Unfortunately, she wasn't a strong swimmer, and she drowned in a deep pool that we still call 'Dorothy's Hole'. Some of you may have noticed the place on the drive in.

"A few years ago, a photographer was taking pictures of the schoolroom here using a film camera. He thought he was alone. When he got his photos developed, however, he beheld the image of a beautiful teenaged girl sitting right in Dorothy's old desk."

A chill cuts through me, and Daphne and I look at each other, jaws hanging.

"Now," Arlis says, "let's all go outside and up the stairs to the Masonic Lodge."

Daphne and I don't say a word as we follow Arlis and the rest of the tourists up the outside stairs. Our guide unlocks a heavy iron-and-glass door, and ushers us into a long room that occupies almost all of the building's second floor.

"Now the Masons," Arlis tells us, "are a fairly secretive society. They probably started as a trades organization way back during the time of King Solomon's Mines. It is no longer just a group for craftsmen, though. It has also become a charitable organization. When they decided to build this building, the Masons saw that they could accomplish two goals. They could build themselves a lodge. They could also provide Bannack's children with a proper school. So they split the building up with the lodge on the top floor and the school on the bottom."

Daphne digs her nails into my bicep, and whispers. *"Slate, this is it! A House Divided!"*

Before I can respond, an older man asks Arlis, "Tell us about the Masonic Lodge number here."

Arlis smiles. "Ah, yes. The number of the Bannack Masonic Lodge is 3-7-77. There have always been a lot of rumors about that number, some of them associated with the vigilante movement. Some people claim that the number represents the dimensions of a person's grave—3 feet wide, 7 feet long, and 77 inches deep. Another theory is that when the vigilantes told you to get out of town, you had 3 hours, 7 minutes, and 77 seconds to skedaddle or they would come after you with the noose. The Masons themselves claim that many of their members were involved in the vigilante movement, though the truth is that many non-Masons participated as well."

"What about this carpet?" someone else asks.

Daphne and I look down to see a long carpet full of strange symbols running down the center of the room. A rope has been set up to keep people from trampling it, and sheets of plastic cover the carpet along its entire length.

"As you can see," Arlis replies, "this carpet has many of the Masonic symbols woven into it. Only the Masons know what a lot of them mean. The plastic has been placed on top of the carpet to keep mice from eating it, but you can see they've already gnawed a few holes in it.

"This, however, is not the original carpet that was in this room. When the Masonic Lodge was closed down in the 1950s, some Masons cut the carpet into two pieces down its center and carted it away. When the Masons began restoring the building in the 1970s, the two halves were returned to the room and placed over to the sides."

Daphne and I look at both sides of the room and, sure enough, spot the two long halves of the original carpet lying against opposite walls.

"The House Divided could also be referring to the carpet," I whisper to Daphne.

Daphne slips her hand into mine, and I find that I'm trembling—though I can't be sure if it's because we've solved the latest clue or because I am holding Daphne's hand. After all, we haven't had much time alone the past couple of days, and there is that unsettled matter of our first kiss still hanging over me.

But no time for that now, Slate, I tell myself.

While the other tourists mill around the large room, Daphne and I immediately start scouring the carpet for the answer to the next part of the riddle,

> *To a House Divided, take this mark,*
> *And count to how a wolf is cloaked.*

I am looking for the number '7' and I am sure Daphne is doing something similar. We barely have a chance to start, though, before Arlis announces, "And now, if you'll finish up with your picture-taking, we'll head on down the street."

Reluctantly, Daphne and I continue on the rest of the tour with Arlis.

"Did you see anything in the carpet?" I ask Daphne, as Arlis walks our tour group down to Bannack's first jail—a dark, horrible-looking shack cleverly decorated with iron rings in the floor to chain down prisoners.

"No," Daphne answers. "I thought there might be a number 7 on the carpet or something like that, but I didn't see it."

"Me neither. And what about the lodge number—3-7-77? Could that be a clue?"

"We've got to get back into that room," Daphne tells me. "Do you think Arlis would let us in later?"

I shrug. "I don't see why not. Maybe we can ask her when this tour is over."

By the time the tour ends, however, Arlis has to leave.

"Sorry, kids," she says. "I'd be happy to let you into that room anytime, but I've got to drive over to Bozeman for a wedding before this storm hits. I'll be back Monday if you want to go in then."

"That would be great," I say, trying to mask my disappointment.

"Yeah, thank you," Daphne says. "Enjoy the wedding."

"I will if I get there!" She smiles, then hurries off down Main Street.

I look up and, for the first time, notice that dark gray clouds have completely blanketed the sky.

"We'd better get back, too," I say.

"Yeah," Daphne agrees. "I'll bet the dads are eager to get out of here."

Nineteen

Sure enough, the dads are pacing like hungry lions when we return to the campground.

"Good, you're here." Dad's voice cracks with impatience.

"We're *early*," I inform him.

"Well, I'm glad. Thanks for getting camp cleaned up. Do you need to go to the bathroom before we head into Dillon?"

"Yes," Daphne and I say together.

"Hurry," Len barks. "The sky's going to open up any second."

Len is right. The first heavy drops start splattering against the OFGOV's windshield as we pull out of the campground. I ride with Len and Daphne while Dad follows, driving our much newer Explorer.

By the time we reach Dillon, the Travelall's windshield wipers race as fast as they can go, but still can't keep up with the sheets of water cascading over the vehicle. Len takes the southern exit and we slosh through streets six inches deep in water. Daphne has to shout to be heard above the rain pounding on the OFGOV's metal roof.

"Where are we staying?"

"The Guesthouse Suites," Len answers, steering

up North Montana Street. "And there might be a surprise waiting for us."

Daphne slaps his shoulder. "What is it?"

Len won't tell.

When we pull into the crowded parking lot, however, I spot a familiar-looking vehicle parked nearby.

I sit up straight.

"Yeah!" Daphne shouts.

Neither of us bothers putting on our rain coats. We bolt out of the OFGOV and rush to the motel lobby, getting soaked in the process. Len and my dad follow us in and ask the motel clerk for our room numbers. Then Daphne and I charge up the stairs to the second floor.

"Sate!" my sister Lily yells when the door opens. She rushes into my arms and quickly, Mom embraces both of us.

Daphne, meanwhile, is hugging her mom Theresa, all of us chuttering like chipmunks by the time Dad One and Dad Two join us, lugging our bags.

"You look bigger," I tell Lily, even though it's only been three weeks since I've seen her.

"I am bigger, but I'm not older until my birthday," she informs me.

We all laugh.

"I'm glad you made it," Dad says to Mom and Theresa. "I started to get worried when I saw how heavy the rain is."

"We left Missoula early," Theresa explains. "The National Weather Service has issued severe thunderstorm warnings all across the state."

"Seems like temperatures have dropped a lot," Mom adds.

"The famous August Singularity," Len muses.

Lily asks, "What's a gust celery?"

We crack up again, but Len explains. "Lily, the August Singularity is when in late summer, an unusual storm system blows through western Montana."

"No one is sure why it happens so regularly," Dad adds, "But it tells us all that Fall is almost here."

I let out a huge sigh. "It also means school is almost here."

"But the leaves will be falling!" Lily shouts.

I grin. It's hard not to share her excitement.

Daphne, Len, and Theresa are sharing a room with two queen-sized beds down the hall, but Dad has gotten us a two-bedroom suite, which is a great place for all of us to hang out while rain pummels the windows and roof outside. Questions fly faster than bolts of lightning as we all try to catch up on the news of the last couple of weeks. Lily starts rummaging around my daypack and discovers the two-way radio.

"What's this?"

"Here, we'll show you," Daphne says, getting Len's and Dad's radios out and showing my sister how they work. I like watching Daphne and Lily together. They're like sisters. Sometimes, I get too impatient with Lily and end up making her cry, but I've never seen Daphne lose her temper with her. She only does that with *me*.

When Daphne finishes explaining, she asks, "Do you want to try them?"

Lily eagerly nods her head. "Are you going to be in there?" she asks, pointing into the radio.

I laugh. "Only her voice will be in there, Lily."

While my sister stays in our suite, Daphne and I split up to different parts of the motel.

"Lily, come in Lily," I say into the radio.

I hear a little electronic squawk, and Dad's voice saying "Just talk into it like a phone, Lily."

"SATE!" Lily yells, almost shattering my ear-drum. "Sate! It's Lily!"

"Not so loud!" I tell her. Then, I hear Daphne joining in on the same frequency. For the next twenty minutes, we roam around the motel, playing with the radios until Dad gets on and says, "Slate, Daphne, return to Base before we get kicked out of the motel for disturbing the other guests. Over."

After all of us shower and put on clean clothes, we pile back into the OFGOV to go out to dinner at Blacktail Station, one of Dillon's fanciest res-taurants. The place has a great Western feel to it, with a stuffed mountain lion greeting us at the entrance, and old-fashioned booths and decorations everywhere. We gorge ourselves on halibut, steak, cheeseburgers and, of course, dessert.

It is still raining after dinner, but the western horizon blazes with tangerine-colored clouds and bands of huckleberry sky. With less than an hour of daylight left, the parents decide to head back to the motel, but I resume contemplating that first kiss.

"Is it okay if we walk back?"

"It's kind of far, isn't it?" Mom asks.

"It's not that far," I say. "Besides, we can take the back way by the fishing pond."

Mom and Theresa look at each other, and I can see relief on Dad's and Len's faces that, for once, they don't have to make the decision.

"Well, if you don't mind getting wet, I guess it's okay," Theresa says.

"I want to come!" Lily says.

"It *is* too far for you," Mom says.

"But I want to!" Lily looks on the verge of tears, but Daphne tells her, "We can play with the radios more when we get back."

"O-okay," Lily submits with a half-sob.

Whew, I think.

After the parents and Lily leave, Daphne and I stroll through downtown before heading back. It delays my plan to kiss her, but I do hold her hand. Besides, Dillon is a neat place, with a lot of funky stores and cafes. After being out in the boonies for so long, it's nice just to feel a city—or at least a town—around us.

We walk by the old courthouse, pass Vigilante Park, and then make our way back toward the railroad tracks to look at the Beaverhead County Museum. The museum is closed, of course, but we read historical signs and snoop around an old sheepherder's wagon on display outside. As we finally decide to start back toward the motel, I begin plotting exactly where along our route I am going to kiss Daphne.

But suddenly, Daphne freezes and hisses, "Look!"

Twenty

Across the street, coming out of a restaurant/casino called Papa T's, I spot a lone figure wearing Carhartt pants. The man quickly pulls the hood of a raincoat over his head, but not before I see a flash of dirty-blonde hair tucked under a dark baseball-style cap.

"Is that...?"

"I think so!" Daphne answers. "What should we do? Go to the police?"

My mind has already slammed into full gear.

"No," I tell her. "They don't believe he's the guy anyway. Let's follow him. See where he goes."

"Do you think that's safe?"

These, of course, are precisely the situations where Daphne needs me most. I grab her arm, look both ways for traffic, and tug her across North Montana Street.

"What if he's got a gun?" Daphne protests.

"This is Montana," I tell her. "Everyone's got a gun. That doesn't mean he's going to shoot at us."

"*I* don't have a gun!"

I roll my eyes. In tight situations, Daphne sometimes loses her sense of humor.

By the time we've crossed the street, the man

is about half a block ahead of us. At the corner of Center Street, he turns right. We hurry to the corner and peek around it just in time to see him go into a place called the Dillon Hotel and Bar.

"C'mon," I say, pulling on Daphne's hand.

We hurry up the street to find not one, but two doors. The second door does indeed lead into the bar, but after a quick glance inside, Daphne and I agree that the man probably entered the first door. I open it and see that this door leads into a narrow hallway with stairs at the end of it. A sign above the door reads "Rooms for Rent".

"Now what?" Daphne asks.

I pull her inside.

"*Slate!*" Daphne objects, but we're already in, our raincoats dripping onto the speckled brown linoleum floor.

Inside the hallway is an open connecting door that leads directly into the bar, and clouds of cigarette smoke pour out of it into the hallway where we stand. The barflies are too busy watching an overhead T.V. to notice us, so I whisper. "Let's go up the stairs."

"Why?" Daphne whispers back.

I lead her forward and, halfway up the stairs, I hear a man's voice. I creep slowly, one step at a time until, peeking just above the level of the second floor, I see the owner of the voice, talking on an actual real-live pay telephone. It's probably the last pay phone in the state of Montana, and I'm surprised someone hasn't grabbed it and put it into a museum.

The phone is mounted on the wall only twenty feet from us. This close, I have no doubt that the man talking is the same guy who tried to scare us away from the mine two days ago.

I turn to Daphne and put my finger to my lips. Then, I tune in to what the man is saying. He's trying to talk quietly, but is clearly upset and his words bounce crisply off of the corridor walls.

"—don't care about the freaking weather! You said you'd be here!"

The man pauses to listen, then answers. "I already told you. That was miles from where I hid them. *No one* is going to find them—not if you get here fast. Besides, if you hadn't rented me that cheap piece-of-crap car, I wouldn't have broken down trying to get out of here and—"

Another pause. Then the man exclaims "*What? You* expect me to hang out in this cow town until *Wednesday?* No way! I'm not doing it. Someone might recognize me and, besides, how would you like to be stuck out here watching the alfalfa grow?"

The man stops talking to listen again, and I notice something moving around inside his mouth against his cheek. It makes him pronounce his words a little strangely.

Probably chewing tobacco, I think to myself. Then, the guy speaks again.

"You'd *better* make it earlier or I might just sell them to someone else."

He pauses again.

"Are you *threatening* me?"

Pause.

"You'd better not be, because with what I know about you, I can bury you, buddy. And just for saying that, you can add another 10% to my fee."

Pause.

"I *am* relaxed. You just get your martini-loving, tuxedo-wearing, cigar-smoking big fat behind out here or—"

And with that, Daphne cracks up laughing.

"Daphne!" I hiss in alarm, but it's too late.

The man's head snaps around to see us both peeking at him from floor level.

"Gotta go!" he shouts and slams the phone down.

"Run!" I holler.

I almost stumble over Daphne as we scramble to the bottom of the stairs.

"Hey you kids! Stop right there!"

I turn to see the man, red-faced start down the stairs after us.

"Go!" I shout.

We fly through the door out into the rain. Daphne starts to turn left, but I seize her hand and tug her hard to the right. "This way!"

"Ow! You don't have to pull my shoulder out of its socket!"

We race down the street and at the corner, I glance back to see the man out on the sidewalk, looking in both directions. Then, our eyes lock and he starts after us.

"STOP! BOTH OF YOU!" he yells again.

We turn right and sprint down North Idaho Street opposite The Bookstore.

"Where are we going?" Daphne pants.

"We don't want him to know where we're staying," I tell her.

I look back again and see that the man has rounded the corner and is gaining on us.

Uh-oh, I think. *At this rate he going to catch us—and soon!*

Then, I get an idea.

"Cross the street!" I tell Daphne.

We glance both ways and cross the road, then hang a quick left onto East Bannack Street. I can hear the man's fast footsteps splashing on the pavement.

"He's gaining on us!" Daphne shouts.

"Don't look back!"

We fly down the block and I can hear that Daphne is right—the man's footsteps are getting closer and closer. *Great,* I think, *just our luck to be chased by the only athletic villain in Montana!*

A trashcan sits on the sidewalk up ahead, and taking a cue from countless movie chase scenes, I knock it over to slow down our pursuer. Unfortunately, it's Daphne, not the bad guy, who trips over the trashcan, and I just barely catch her before she sprawls to the sidewalk.

"What are you *doing?*" she cries, regaining her feet.

"Sorry! Keep running!"

Thanks to my stupid trashcan stunt, only fifteen yards now separate us from the man chasing us. We tear across another street and I can almost feel the man's strong hands seizing my neck.

But before that happens, I see what I've been looking for.

"There it is!" I shout.

With a desperate surge of energy, we sprint across one last street and finally, I hear the footsteps falter behind us.

And for good reason.

Just up ahead, on the left side of the courthouse, is the well-lit sign for the Dillon Police and Beaverhead County Sheriff's Office. As I yank open the office door, I glance back to see the man, standing in the shadows across the street. He glares at us furiously, then quickly turns away.

Twenty-One

"You kids alright?"

Daphne and I look over at a male sheriff's deputy sitting behind the glass reception window fifteen feet away. Our legs are completely drenched and the water running off us is forming small reservoirs at our feet.

Daphne flashes the deputy a relieved smile. "We are now."

"Say, aren't you the kids who led us on that wild-goose chase near Bannack yesterday?"

I can feel my face turn red. "Uh, yes sir. That would be us."

"Well, what are you doing here now?"

It occurs to me that after the wild-goose incident, maybe Daphne and I should keep our mouths shut about what just happened. Daphne, of course, reaches a different conclusion.

"The same man we saw at the mine just chased us across town!" she exclaims.

"What?" The deputy stands up so quickly, he almost tips his chair backward onto the floor. "Here, let's get you kids dried off. Verna!"

A woman wearing a police uniform enters the reception area through a side door. After quickly sizing up the situation, she leads us back into the inner office area, where she gets us towels and tries to make us comfortable in an unoccupied room. Meanwhile, I hear the deputy—whose name is Rick—make a couple of phone calls from another room. Which reminds me.

"Uh, Verna," I say. "We should give our parents a call and tell them we're all right."

"Sure, Hon," Verna says. "Just hit the extension 4 button to dial out."

When I tell Mom where we are, she responds predictably.

"You're *where?*"

Without going into every detail, I explain over the phone that Daphne and I decided to drop by the police/sheriff's station. "We remembered a couple of other things about our experience at the mine that they might want to know," I say. "It'll only take a little while."

"We'll be over right this minute," Mom says, in full alarm mode.

"No! I mean, no. They will give us a ride as soon as we're finished."

"Slate, I don't like this!"

"It's okay, Mom. Really. We'll be back in an hour or so."

Reluctantly, Mom hangs up the phone. Moments later, our favorite FBI man, Agent Bullock walks through the door.

He regards us without so much as a 'hello' or 'what's up?', and then asks Rick, the deputy sheriff, what's going on. After Rick explains everything, Bullock tells him, "I guess you'd better send a man over to the rooming house to see if we can find this guy."

"We're already on it," Rick says.

Agent Bullock nods. Then, finally, he turns his attention to us. He pulls up a seat and asks us to again explain exactly what happened. Tonight, he's not wearing his dark sunglasses—though I'm sure he would like to—and to his credit, he listens closely to what we have to say.

"So," he says, when Daphne and I have finished our story. "You didn't hear this man specifically mention the paintings or art, is that correct?"

"That's right," I say.

"But it definitely sounded like he was trying to unload something illegal," Daphne joins in.

"But neither of you heard him say exactly what he was talking about?"

Reluctantly, we shake our heads. "It was more of a hunch," I say, weakly.

I expect Bullock to dismiss us, but again, he surprises me. "Well, sometimes a hunch is all you've got to go on."

And just like that, I am liking this guy a little better.

"But," he continues, "it's also possible that the

man was simply mad at you for eavesdropping on his conversation, right?"

"It's possible," Daphne says. "But I think something else was going on."

I note that Daphne has again adopted her slightly flirty voice, and I can feel the needle rising on my Annoyed Meter. Then, I remind myself that Daphne really can't help herself. Flirting is just something hard-wired into her—like cracking bad jokes and reading romantic vampire books.

I try not to take it personally.

"Well," Agent Bullock concludes. "We'll see if the police and sheriffs can find this guy. If so, maybe we can get to the bottom of this."

Just then, Verna arrives with some donuts, milk, and coffee. "Anyone like a snack while we're waiting?"

"Yeah!" Daphne and I exclaim.

With Agent Bullock, we dig into the goodies.

"I really shouldn't be eating these things," the FBI man says. "It's probably the worst hazard of being in law enforcement."

Both Daphne and I laugh.

"So," Daphne asks, selecting a fat jelly donut. "How long have you been working on this Charlie Russell case?"

Agent Bullock leans back in his chair and bites into a chocolate-covered old-fashioned. "I volunteered for the case about two years ago," he tells us. "I actually studied art in college."

I stop chewing for a split-second. "You did?" It's the last thing I expect to hear from a suit-wearing, dark sunglasses-loving FBI man.

Bullock snorts. "Hard to believe, huh? After college, I couldn't get a job so I decided to go through FBI training. To my surprise, I found that I liked investigative work. When this case came up, nobody else wanted it, so I put my name in. I expected to solve it a lot faster than this."

"Do you like Russell?" Daphne asks, trying to keep jelly from dripping all over her shirt.

Agent Bullock takes a sip of coffee and considers the question.

"Not at first," he admits. "Russell was mostly self-taught, you know, and a lot of his early work, especially with mixing colors, is pretty crude. He improved over time, though, and more than that, I've come to admire what he was trying to do."

"My mom is an artist," I brag. "She says that Russell got to Montana just as everything was changing."

Bullock again nods. "He came out to live the dream of the Wild West. Then, when he got here, he discovered it was all disappearing. The buffalo were wiped out. The Indians had been defeated and forced onto reservations. The open range gave way to farms and homesteads. Russell kind of made it his mission to record that vanishing way of life before it was lost forever."

"You really know a lot about him," Daphne says.

Bullock stares at his hands. "Not entirely on purpose. Since this case started, I've pretty much been living and breathing Charles M. Russell."

Then, he swallows and turns his eyes to Daphne. "So to answer your original question, I didn't start out liking Russell. But now I'd have to say that I'm one of his biggest fans."

Just then, a couple of police officers come into the office. Bullock stands. "Did you find anything?"

The first officer shakes his head. "We checked out the hotel and asked around the Dillon Bar. A couple of the customers remembered seeing the guy go in and out of the place, but he's definitely not staying in any of the rooms. It appears he went there just to use the phone."

"Okay," Bullock says. "Thanks, guys."

"We've put out a description of him and will pick him up if we see him," the second officer adds.

After the policemen leave, Agent Bullock says, "Well, looks like we're back to Square One."

"So you don't think the guy that chased us is involved with the art museum robbery?" Daphne asks.

Bullock shrugs. "Right now, we just don't have evidence that points in that direction. My guess is no. It sounds like he was probably just some guy who got mad at you for listening in on his phone call. I know I wouldn't like a couple of kids eaves-dropping on me."

Daphne and I exchange sheepish grins.

"It's still good that you let us know what hap-pened, though. Come on, I'll give you a ride back to your motel."

Twenty-Two

By the next morning the storm has passed, and all of us—including Theresa, Lily, and Mom—are heading back to Bannack.

"Lily's been pestering me to go camping, so we tossed our camping gear in the back when we left home," Mom explains, as we caravan out of Dillon. "Besides, after the events of the last couple of days, Theresa and I feel better keeping close to our kids."

After Daphne and I got back to the motel last night, we tried to downplay our latest experience with 'Mr. Carhartt'. Our parents, however, saw through our story.

"Even though you said that man was mad at you for listening to him on the phone, it sounds a little more worrisome than that," Mom insists from our minivan's driver's seat.

"I agree," Theresa joins in from the front passenger seat. Up ahead, I can see Dad driving our Explorer, and ahead of that, Len driving the OFGOV.

"But really," Daphne says, tucking a strand of black hair behind her ear. "The more I think about it, the more I think maybe Slate and I overreacted. That maybe this guy just wanted to talk to us."

"Yeah," I lie.

Theresa turns around and gives Daphne a look that says she's not buying it.

The problem, of course, is that Daphne and I don't buy it either. Mr. Carhartt was definitely *after* us. And even if nobody else believes us, we both think the guy had something to do with the museum robbery. Unfortunately, there's not a thing we can do about it anymore. Mr. Carhartt is probably long-gone by now, and the sheriff's and police departments made it clear they'd wasted enough time on the guy. Before dropping us off last night, in fact, Agent Bullock told us that if nothing else happened on the case in the next day or so, he was going to be heading back to D.C.

I think to myself, *So that pretty much wraps it up for the Charlie Russell robberies.*

Fortunately, Daphne and I still have something to keep us occupied. It's spelled T-R-E-A-S-U-R-E.

As soon as we reclaim our camping spots in Bannack and help get the tents set back up, Daphne announces, "We're going to walk into Bannack."

"I want to come!" Lily shouts.

"So do we," Theresa says.

I roll my eyes at Daphne. "Well, uh," I say, "we're really just going to poke around."

"That's okay. We like to poke around, too."

There's nothing Daphne and I can say, so fifteen minutes later, while the dads head back out into the hills, the five of us tromp down to the ghost town. The ground is still soggy from last night's rains, but the sun has started to peek out from clouds, and it looks like it's going to be a nice afternoon.

"Let's go to the visitor's center," Mom suggests.

Lily is walking between Daphne and me, holding each of our hands. She shouts, "Yeah. Let's go to the vis-tor center. I want a stuffed monkey!"

"You are a stuffed monkey," I tell her.

"One-two-three...Weee!" Daphne shouts and together, we swing Lily up into the air.

While our moms and Lily snoop around the gift shop, Daphne and I talk to Susan, the visitor's center manager.

Like the rest of the park staff, she knows us pretty well by now. "How are you two?" she asks.

"Pretty good," I tell her.

"Did you stay dry last night?"

"We got a motel room in town," Daphne explains.

"Smart move."

"Say," I ask, "Arlis didn't happen to come back early, did she?"

Susan shakes her head. "No, but is there anything I can help you with?"

"Well, we wanted to take another look at the Masonic Lodge. We thought it was pretty neat, but didn't have much time there during the tour yesterday."

Daphne holds up her camera. "I wanted to get some pictures."

"Oh, that shouldn't be a problem. Let me see if Tom or John are in."

Susan picks up a phone and dials an extension. "Tom? Slate and Daphne—the two kids staying down at the campground—were wondering if they could get into the Masonic Lodge for a few minutes."

Susan nods and says "Uh-huh" a couple of times, and then hangs up the phone.

"He said it wouldn't be any problem. Just meet him next door and he'll walk you over."

"Thanks," I tell her.

Daphne lets our moms know we're just going to step out for a bit.

"That's okay," Theresa says. "We're not quite done shopping. We'll meet you out on the street somewhere."

After we leave the visitor's center, I hold up my hand for a high five. "Good job lying."

Daphne slaps my palm. "Piece of cake."

Tom is the park historian and he's already outside by the time we reach the street. "Morning," he greets us. "So you're interested in the lodge building, eh?"

"We just saw a lot of cool stuff in there," Daphne tells him, as we begin walking down Main Street. "I thought it would be fun to take some pictures."

"I understand that," he says. "I've been here almost twenty years and haven't even come close to learning everything I want to about this place."

We reach the lodge/schoolhouse, and Tom leads us up the outside steps to the second floor. He unlocks the heavy door and steps aside so we can enter.

Once inside, Daphne and I immediately walk over to the carpet running down the room's center.

"Tom?" Daphne asks. "You don't know what any of these symbols mean, do you?"

"'Fraid not. A lot of them go way back. I'm sure a real Mason could probably tell you some of them—if he wasn't sworn to secrecy or something."

Then, he points to a wall. "But see? A lot of the same symbols in the carpet are on that big poster there."

Daphne and I follow his finger to a large poster with all kinds of strange symbols under headings such as "Master Mason" and "Fellow Craft" and "Entered Apprentice".

"We didn't even see that before," Daphne says, raising her camera to her eye.

"Anything else I can do for you today?" Tom asks.

"No. No thank you," I tell him. "This is great."

"Well, here's the key. Do me a favor and lock up after you're done. Drop the key off back at the office."

"We will," Daphne says. "Thank you."

"Don't mention it. I'm always glad to see young people taking an interest in history."

If you only knew, I think.

Twenty-Three

After Tom leaves, I pull out the paper with our clues and read,

> To a House Divided, take this mark,
> And count to how a wolf is cloaked.
>
> And with that precious knowledge stored,
> Find the dwelling of one once adored.

"Okay," I say, "so we've got the mark."

"The number '7'," Daphne confirms.

"Right. So what do we do with it?"

"Something about how a wolf is cloaked. What could that be? Fur? Hair? A cape like in Little Red Riding Hood?"

We look all around the room, but keep coming back to the big chart of Masonic symbols on the wall.

"What are you?" Daphne muses. Then, suddenly, she starts laughing.

I elbow her. "What?"

She directs my attention to the bottom of the chart, to a column with seven symbols in it. "Look," she says, pointing to the last symbol.

I slap my forehead. "That's so obvious!" I tell her.

The last of the seven symbols in the column is a little drawing of a sheep.

"A wolf in sheep's clothing," Daphne quotes.

I grin. "But what do we do with it?"

Daphne takes the sheet of clues from me. "So with this sheep, we have to find the house of someone who was very popular here. And we already know it wasn't Henry Plummer."

"We don't know that," I correct her. "All we know is that his house doesn't exist anymore."

"True," Daphne admits. "But Plummer wasn't 'adored' for that long. I mean, they took him out and hanged him, didn't they?"

"Well, there is *that* small detail."

"I think the clue is talking about somebody else."

"Okay, All-Knowing One, but who?"

Daphne tucks a strand of hair behind her ear and adopts her serious sleuthing voice. "Well," she begins.

And suddenly, I just can't believe how cute and smart Daphne looks. Her hair is slightly messy. Her green eyes are blazing. When a whiff of her peach-scented shampoo hits my nostrils, my heart starts pounding and the room starts wobbling. Before Daphne can finish her sentence, I lurch forward and mash my lips against hers.

I'll bet you didn't see that coming, did you?

Neither did I—and neither did Daphne, judging by how still she has suddenly become.

The seconds tick by, and our lips remain firmly planted together. The only problem is, I am not sure what to do next.

For weeks, I have devoted every thought and brain cell toward getting enough courage to kiss Daphne. Unfortunately, I haven't spent nearly as much time figuring out *how* to kiss her. I guess I thought that once I made *the move*, everything would pretty much happen by itself.

Albert Einstein would call that a serious miscalculation.

Arms dangling like limp worms at our sides, it is suddenly very obvious that neither Daphne nor I have any idea what to do next. I feel Daphne's lips twitch a little bit, and my own twitch back.

But what now? I ask my brain.

No response.

Thanks a lot, brain.

Without any other options, I pull back and look at Daphne.

Her eyes stare back at me. She doesn't smile, but she doesn't frown either. She looks like she's holding her breath, but her face doesn't reveal anything. Now, I am feeling afraid.

What if she didn't want me to kiss her? I ask myself. *What if I've just made a colossal mistake?*

I wait for Daphne to respond, my whole life resting in her hands.

And she drops it.

Instead of giving me even the slightest encouragement, she exhales, breaks eye contact and, in a slightly shaky voice, says, "Uh, a lot of, uh, people could have been kissed—I mean, *liked*—here in, uh, Bannack."

Where's Daphne? I ask myself. *Where's that girl who, just a month ago, told me it was okay if I liked her?*

She has disappeared.

Daphne continues blathering about who the 'one once adored' could be in the treasure clue, but I am no longer listening. The room we're standing in seems a little darker—and a lot more confusing—than it did just a minute ago.

Twenty-Four

We leave the Masonic Lodge, lock the door, and silently walk back to the park headquarters to return the key to Tom.

"You find what you wanted?"

"We think so," Daphne tells him. "Can we ask you a question, though?"

Tom leans back in his vinyl office chair. "Fire away."

"We were wondering if there was anyone really popular in Bannack?"

Tom's eyebrows lift. "Popular?"

"You know," Daphne elaborates. "Someone who lived here a long time ago that people, well, *adored*."

Daphne glances at me for some help, but since our kiss—or rather, since Daphne's *reaction* to our kiss—I'm not feeling overly chatty.

"Hm..." Tom begins tapping a pen on his desk while pondering the question. "There were certainly popular people here. Mabel Ovitt comes to mind. She ran the store down the street—Number 17 in the guide. She wrote a book about the vigilantes and was actually the last person living in Bannack."

"When did she die?" Daphne asks.

"I'm pretty sure it was 1968," Tom tells her.

"She had stopped her car to open a gate one day, and the car somehow rolled back and crushed her. She's buried in the new cemetery outside of town."

"That's terrible!" Daphne exclaims.

What's terrible, I think, *is when you spend months trying to kiss somebody, and when you finally do, you find out she didn't even want you to!*

Tom nods. "It is terrible. Do you think it might be her you're thinking of?"

Daphne chews at her lip and shakes her head. "I don't think so. We were thinking of someone who maybe lived longer ago. Besides, she didn't have a brick house, did she?"

"To my knowledge, no-one in Bannack owned a brick house," Tom says. "Unless you're thinking of the hotel down the street?"

"No..."

"Sorry I can't be of more help, but if I think of anything, I'll let you know."

"Thank you," Daphne says.

"Yeah. Thanks," I mutter.

Back out on the street, Daphne asks, "Well, do you have any more ideas on who the 'one once adored' might be?"

I don't look at her. "No."

"Hm. Well, I guess we should try to find the moms and Lily."

"You go ahead," I tell her. "I'm going to take a walk."

I can feel Daphne's eyes on me. "Really? Do you want me to come with you?"

"I think I'll go alone," I say, and begin heading across the street.

"Slate?"

I wheel around. *"What?"*

Daphne and I are standing about ten feet apart. Her eyes bore into me with a pleading look, though I'm not sure why.

"What?" I ask again, unsuccessfully trying to soften my tone.

Daphne's shoulders slump and she drops her eyes. "Nothing."

I march across the street and past the site of the first Governor's Mansion. Behind it, I follow a little path to a footbridge that leads over Grasshopper Creek. Normally, I would stop to stare into the peaceful, clear stream to see if I could spot any trout. Today, I am too steamed up for that. At a fast clip, I cross the bridge and cut through the area once known as Yankee Flats. Mining activities totally obliterated the houses that used to stand here, but it has been transformed into the park's group picnic area.

As I walk, I replay the kiss in the Masonic Lodge, wondering if I did anything wrong.

No, I conclude. I mean, I probably wasn't as smooth as Romeo or one of the male vampires in the books Daphne loves so much.

"But give me a break," I mutter. "It was my first kiss. For a mere mortal, I thought I did pretty good."

Inside, though, I'm not feeling so confident. What I really think is that I must have messed up something for Daphne to act the way she did. Maybe I should have read the book *First Kisses for Idiots* before I went and smashed my lips against Daphne's, but it's too late for that now.

On the other side of the picnic area, I come to the dirt road that cuts a wide circle around Bannack to the town's east side. Without thinking, I turn left, toward the Bannack Mill.

Since I arrived in Bannack, I have been meaning to walk over to the mill, but with Dad's work schedule, I just haven't gotten around to it. I did read an interesting article about the mill in the visitor's center, however.

During its heyday, Bannack's mills filled the canyon with noise day and night. The mills crushed the rock, or ore, containing the gold and silver. Then, they used different methods to extract the precious metals. The Hendricks Mill—as the Bannack Mill used to be called—started as a crude crushing facility in the 1800s. Different owners upgraded the mill to make it more efficient, but most couldn't turn a profit. By 1971, the mill closed for good.

After that, the buildings were vandalized and the building that housed the rock crushing machines burned down. As I walk up the road, however, I can still see the large building that remains. As I get closer, I also begin to pass huge, rusted metal machine parts—pieces of the crushing machines, I'm guessing—sitting half-hidden among the sagebrush.

When I reach the dirt road that leads to the remaining building, I am stopped by a fence and a gate. Large signs shout, "No Trespassing! Danger! Keep Out!"

I halt and look at the mill through the fence. Even from a hundred yards away, I can feel the history—and mystery—of the place. The building looks like it's built of old cedar or pine, and has aged to wonderful burnt orange and yellow colors. From where I stand, the open east end reveals several huge, redwood vats, each at least ten or fifteen feet tall.

Those must be the tanks where they used cyanide to pull out the gold, I think to myself.

My impulse is to just climb over the fence and sneak into the place for a closer look, but the warning signs keep me rooted in place.

The mill probably is dangerous, after all, I think. Even if the building isn't about to fall down, the chemicals that were used—and released—by the mining activities were no laughing matter.

I am about to turn away and keep walking when my eye catches something on the ground. It's another piece of litter and, as usual, I reach down to pick it up.

"Idiot," I mutter to the person who dropped it.

I start to shove the trash into my pocket, when my hand freezes and I look at it again.

I can almost hear the giant CLUNK as the missing puzzle piece falls into place. My mouth opens and I quietly exclaim, *"Holy Cyanide!"*

Twenty-Five

Iturn and race back toward our campground with only one thought in mind: *I've got to tell Daphne!* I only hope that after I was such a jerk to her, she hasn't gone waltzing off somewhere else. Today, though, at least some luck shines down on me. When I jog gasping into the campground, I find her playing solitaire at our camp picnic table.

"Daphne!" I shout.

Her head jerks up.

"What...?"

"Where are our moms and Lily?"

"Still looking around Bannack. Why?"

"Look what I found." I reach into my pocket and hand her the piece of litter I picked up.

She examines it for a moment and then looks at me. "It's a Jolly Rancher candy wrapper. So?"

I put my hands on my knees, still panting. "It's...not just a Jolly Rancher candy wrapper. It's a *watermelon* Jolly Rancher candy wrapper."

She glances back at the wrapper, then returns her eyes to me. "Again, so?"

I groan. "Don't you *get* it?"

"Get what? That you really want a piece of candy right now?"

Daphne stares at me as if I've gone certifiably crazy. And that's when I realize—I never told her about the first candy wrapper I found up at the mine that day.

"Oh!" I slap my forehead and quickly sit down to explain. When I finish, she says, "Wait. So let me recap. You think that because you found two candy wrappers—"

"Two *Jolly Rancher watermelon* flavor wrappers."

"Right. Two Jolly Rancher watermelon wrappers, you think that means that the stolen art from the university museum is hidden near here?"

"It's not only the wrappers," I tell her. "When we were watching Mr. Carhartt on the phone, he kept moving something around in his mouth. At the time, I thought he was chewing tobacco, but I could hear a faint clicking sound, like something hard knocking against his teeth. I could swear that I caught a faint whiff of a fruity odor, too."

"A *Jolly Rancher* fruity odor."

I nod enthusiastically. "That's right."

"Which only leaves a gap in logic that's about, what, ten times as wide as the Grand Canyon?"

"No! No! No! Don't you get it?" I am practically shouting now. "This guy is super smart. You know how he went into that boarding house to use the phone?"

"Yeeeees."

"Well, he used that phone, but he wasn't staying

there! He was making sure that anyone looking for him was thrown off the scent. He did the same thing with his car."

"You mean the Ford Taurus they found abandoned fifteen miles from here?"

"That's right! He abandoned his car way across the county so people would look for him over there instead of where he really is."

"Slate," Daphne says, "Why would he go to all that trouble? Why not just store the stolen paintings in a motel room in Dillon? Or get a different car and leave the county?"

"Don't you remember his phone conversation?" I ask. "His first car broke down somewhere. By the time he got another one—"

"The Ford Taurus."

"Probably. But the point is, by the time he was actually heading out of town, the roadblocks were already up. What I figure is that he tried to make his escape on Hwy 278 that runs past Bannack here. He probably planned to drive through the Big Hole over to the Bitterroot Valley, and from there, down to Idaho or even up to Missoula."

"So why didn't he?"

"He probably saw a highway patrol car up ahead and turned left off the highway onto a dirt road. You saw the maps. Almost all of those dirt roads lead up and over a pass, right past the mine where Mr. Carhartt confronted us a couple of days ago."

Finally, Daphne's expression begins to soften. "So you think he put the art—"

I complete her sentence. "Yes! He put the paintings in the mine we found when we were collecting rock samples for our dads. That's why he tried so hard to scare us away."

"And you're saying that after he saw us snooping around, he moved all the paintings, but not too far."

"He couldn't have taken them far. With cops crawling all over the place, he had to move fast, but couldn't risk being seen. Now, he's just hiding out, waiting for Mr. Big—the guy who hired him—to fly out to pick up the paintings and pay him off."

Daphne is now looking like she might believe my story.

"And where do you think he's stashed them while he's waiting?"

"I don't know for sure, but judging by this Jolly Rancher wrapper, maybe over near the Bannack Mill."

Daphne takes a deep breath. "And I suppose you want to go look for them."

"Of course I want to go look for them!"

"Don't you think we should call the police or sheriff?"

I drop my eyes. "Well, uh…"

Daphne smirks. "Admit it, Slate. Even you think this idea is far-fetched."

"*No!*" I straighten my posture. "It's the only idea

that makes sense. It's just that after we already raised the alarm twice, I want to make sure I'm right this time."

Daphne presses her finger against her cheek in a mock pose. "Hm...this sounds like a story I've heard before. Something about not crying wolf..."

"Very funny. So," I say impatiently. "Are you going to help me?"

"You mean am I going to let you help *me*?"

"Huh?" Then, I get it and grin. "Right. So are you going to let me help you?"

Daphne flashes me a quick, dazzling smile, but then exchanges it for her "all business" face.

"Let's go," she says.

Twenty-Six

We leave a note for the moms that we'll be back in a couple of hours and throw water and headlamps into our daypacks. Then, we head toward the Bannack Mill.

"So do you have any idea where to look?" Daphne asks as we walk along the dirt bypass road that circles Bannack.

"Just up the hill from the mill is the hardrock mine where they got the ore from," I tell her.

"But I thought that most of the gold here came from placer deposits?"

"It did. Giant dredges were set up right in Grasshopper Creek to dig up the gravel deposits from the valley and separate the gold out. But you know how gold strikes go. The miners know that the placer gold is washing down into the stream from a vein of ore higher up in the rock. So once the placer deposits are discovered, miners look for those original veins."

Daphne nods. "The mother lode."

"Yep. The problem with Bannack is that they never found a big giant mother lode like they found in a lot of other mining areas. That's a big reason why Bannack kind of emptied out when they found gold in Virginia City a few months after the find here."

"But they must have found something in Bannack or they wouldn't have built the mills to process the ore."

"They did," I tell her. "I'm just saying those operations were not as successful as they were in other places."

Soon, we are back at the locked gate that leads to the mill. Daphne reads the warning signs I read earlier. "Geez, they really don't want people going in, do they? Do you think Mr. Carhartt could be hiding the paintings in there?"

"I don't think so," I tell her. "The mill is still owned and managed by Bannack State Park, and they give tours there every weekend. He probably wouldn't want to risk any park people snooping around."

"So what now?"

I point up the overgrown remains of a dirt road. "I think the mine is up there. Let's go take a look."

Daphne reaches for my arm. "Slate, maybe this isn't such a good idea. What if that guy is up there right now?"

The thought had occurred to me, but I'd quickly dismissed it. "It's broad daylight," I tell Daphne, sweeping my hand across the dazzling Montana sky. "If he was going to come here at all, it would be at night. Besides, you heard his phone conversation.

Mr. Carhartt's boss, Mr. Big, said he wasn't going to be able to come out until Wednesday. That's three days from now."

Daphne still looks doubtful. "I guess you're right."

We follow the old dirt road that slopes up through the sagebrush until it reaches another, better dirt road. Even though the sun is out now, the ground is still wet from last night's storm, and we have to stop several times to scrape sticky gumbo off our shoes. While we do that, I notice that the entire area surrounding us has been scarred by old mining activities. It's as if giant prairie dogs or gophers have dug up and overturned every square inch of the mountainside. But then we arrive at what really interests us—the horizontal mining tunnel bored into the side of the mountain.

A steel grating covers the mine entrance, and standing in front of it, Daphne and I can feel the cool air washing out of the mine from deep inside the mountain. "Look," Daphne says, picking up a twisted steel padlock. "This looks like it's been cut off."

"Mr. Carhartt probably did that himself. C'mon, let's go in."

Daphne again grabs my arm. "Slate, look at the sign."

Right next to the mine entrance is a large sign explaining that mines are extremely dangerous and for everyone to stay out. Our dads' warnings about mines also echo in my head. On the other hand, this mine looks fairly stable.

I take out my headlamp and put it on. Flashing the beam into the tunnel, I say, "It looks like they did a good job shoring up the entrance with wooden beams."

"Slate, those beams might be a hundred years old."

"Not a hundred. If the mine still operated in the 1960s, that would make them—"

"Fifty years old," Daphne says. "That's *half a century!*"

"That's not so old when you really think about it."

Daphne puts her hand on her hip and gives me the ole' Irritated Frog. "You know what I mean. Would our dads tell us to go in there?"

"Uh, no," I admit. "But the question is, would they go in there themselves?"

"They're professional geologists!"

"And we're professional geologists' *children!* Come on," I urge her. "We'll just go in a little ways. If we don't find anything within, say, fifty yards, we'll come right back out."

Daphne growls, but unslings her pack and also puts on her headlamp. "I'm only doing this to look after you," she grumps.

I grin and think, *Chock up another one for Slate Stephens' Super Powers of Persuasion.*

Daphne and I have both actually been in mines with our fathers before, and as we enter, the familiar smells of dust and rock seep into my nose. For the first few yards, the mineshaft floor is soft and muddy.

"Look," Daphne says, pointing to the ground. "Footprints. Someone's been here recently."

I study them. "These footprints don't look that new," I say. "I didn't see any prints right outside, did you?"

"I wasn't looking."

I shrug and we keep walking. On the floor around us are a few mining artifacts including rusted iron cans and nails, and wooden beams.

Something catches Daphne's eye, and she bends over to pick it up. "Look," she says, handing it to me.

My pulse quickens. "Another Jolly Ranger wrapper! *Watermelon!* Now do you believe me?"

"I'm starting to."

We've walked about thirty yards into the mine, and the light from the opening is starting to grow dim. I readjust the beam on my headlamp, and we both continue slowly forward. The tunnel is raw now, with no wooden beams to support it. We've traveled beyond the loose surface soils of the mountain, and are entering solid bedrock, where supports aren't as necessary. With each step, though, I feel my mouth getting drier and my nerves jumpier. I glance over at Daphne and see her jaw clenched tight.

After about a hundred yards, the mine tunnel widens into a little room.

"Look here!" Daphne whispers.

She shines her headlamp into an alcove—really more like a narrow crack—carved into the mineshaft wall. "Something's in here," she says.

"Garbage bags," I observe.

"With something inside of them."

While I stand guard, Daphne reaches into the crack and pulls out the objects. Then, I shine my headlamp on the first one while Daphne opens it.

"*Paintings!*" she exclaims.

They aren't the Charlie Russell paintings. In fact, I don't even recognize them, but I have no doubt they came from the University of Montana Western art museum.

"I can't believe we found them," Daphne adds, starting in on the second package.

One by one, Daphne unwraps the other packages—three of them altogether—each containing two or three pieces of art. When she's all finished, we stand back and look at them leaning against the mineshaft wall. Then, we look at each other.

"Where are the Russell paintings?" I ask.

Daphne tucks a strand of her hair behind her ear. "They're not here."

"No they're not," we hear a man's voice say behind us.

We both spin around and shine our headlamps on a figure holding his own flashlight.

Mr. Carhartt.

Twenty-Seven

"I knew you kids were trouble," Mr. Carhartt growls. "Turn off those flashlights."

Daphne turns off her headlamp, but as I reach for mine, my hand shakes so badly that I fumble at the switch. Mr. Carhartt impatiently reaches forward, rips it off my head, slams it to the ground, and grinds the bulb under his heel. Then, he shines his own light directly into our faces.

"Do you mind?" Daphne tells him, holding her hand up in front of her eyes.

"I *do* mind," Mr. C. says. "I mind a lot! Why are you kids sticking your noses into my business?"

"This isn't *your* business," Daphne tells him. "These paintings don't belong to you."

I look over at her, amazed she is able to talk— and so brazenly. Then again, that's one reason we make such a good team. While I'm good at getting us into situations, Daphne is better at talking our way out of them.

"They belong to me now," says Mr. Carhartt. "And there's not a thing you two can do about it."

Finally, I find my voice. "W-we already called the sheriff before we came up here. They'll be here any minute."

Mr. C. laughs. "Oh, right. With all the telephones around here, I should probably just turn and run right now."

I ignore the sarcasm.

"Who are you working for?" Daphne asks.

The question catches Mr. Carhartt off-guard and he stiffens. "I work for myself."

"No you don't," says Daphne. "You don't look like the kind of person to take an interest in art. Otherwise you wouldn't have left so many valuable pieces behind in the museum."

I again look over at Daphne and think, *How does she know what got left behind?*

But if she's bluffing, it works, because Mr. Carhartt's tone gets defensive. "I didn't *want* any of the other pieces, including these here," he says, waving at the paintings leaning against the tunnel wall. "I took these other paintings to confuse anybody looking for me, but I only wanted the two Russells."

"Because that's what your boss told you to get?"

"That's right!" Then, realizing he just admitted he has a boss, he shouts, "I mean no! Enough of this! You kids keep your traps shut while I figure out what to do with you."

Mr. C. reaches into his pocket and pulls out a Jolly Rancher candy and sticks it into his mouth.

"A-hem! Aren't you going to offer us one?" Daphne asks. "Just because you're a crook and a litterbug, doesn't mean you can't have some manners."

Again, I am impressed by Daphne's boldness, but it also worries me a little. If she goes too far...what's that phrase, out of the pot and into the frying pan?

But Mr. Carhartt grunts, reaches back into his pocket, and tosses two candies on the ground in front of us. We stoop to pick them up.

Daphne looks at hers and frowns. "Don't you have any grape?"

"Geez, kid, you're pushing your luck. Take the darned candy or give it back."

"It's just that I'm allergic to the food coloring they use for the watermelon," Daphne says. "Last year I had to go to the hospital because I'd eaten—"

"Okay! Okay!" Mr. Carhartt tells her. "I don't need your entire medical history."

He reaches back into his pocket, and this time pulls out a whole handful of Jolly Ranchers. "Pick what you want," he tells us, extending his hand.

We both step forward and suddenly, I spot an opportunity. As Daphne reaches for a new candy, I notice that Mr. Carhartt has tucked his flashlight loosely under his arm. In a moment of inspiration, I swing my hand down hard against the end of the flashlight. Sure enough, it clatters to the floor of the tunnel and the bulb goes out.

"RUN!" I shout.

Daphne and I both dodge around Mr. C. and sprint toward the tiny circle of light at the mine entrance. I stumble on a wooden beam and sprawl to the ground, but my adrenaline pops me back up in a flash, Daphne ahead of me.

We hear Mr. Carhartt cursing behind us, and then footsteps running in pursuit. We have about a twenty-yard head start, but I already know how fast Mr. Carhartt can run. Chances are slim-to-none we're going to make it to the mine opening before he catches us. As I pass three lengths of old iron rail leaning against the mine wall, however, I decide to try the old movie trick one more time. I pull the rails down behind me and to my astonishment, it works! I hear Carhartt catch his feet on the rails and tumble with a clatter behind me. His howls echo through the tunnel and he yells things I'd better not repeat until we're all *much* older.

With Mr. C. still cursing behind us, we reach the mouth of the mine and, without hesitating, dash down the dirt road.

"HELP!" Daphne shouts at the top of her lungs.

"HELP!" I yell, hoping someone will hear us.

I glance back to see Mr. C.'s pomegranate face emerge from the mine, but he is limping so badly that my hopes for escape suddenly soar.

Daphne and I cut off the newer dirt road, and hop and scramble down the older, overgrown one. We quickly cover the quarter mile of sagebrush to the Bannack Mill, crowing for help all the way.

As we reach the entrance to the Mill, we spot a man in a park service cap standing next to the gate. The gate is now open, and he motions us toward the mill. "Quick! This way!"

Daphne follows his direction, and I am so relieved to see another adult, I also follow without thinking. We keep running, covering the last hundred yards of the dirt access road until we reach the lone, remaining mill building.

It's not until I am standing next to the huge redwood cyanide vats inside the building, panting next to Daphne, that I finally think, *This is strange. Why did this guy urge us toward the mill?*

"Whew!" Daphne tells me.

"You can say that again."

"Whew!"

Instead of calling her on the bad joke, I hug her, and then we both wait for the man in the cap to join us.

"Are we glad to see you!" Daphne tells him as he walks up to us.

I expect the man to be smiling, but instead he scowls. Studying him more closely, I see he is older, maybe in his early sixties, with gray hair and pale skin I wouldn't expect to see on a park ranger. Then, I read his cap. It's not actually a ranger cap, I realize, but a green tourist cap from Yellowstone National Park.

"Hey," I say. "Who are you?"

Daphne looks confused, glancing at me and then at the man.

And that's when we see Mr. Carhartt, eyes blazing, limping up the dirt access road toward us.

Twenty-Eight

"**Y**ou punks!" Mr. Carhartt shouts, coming into the building. He pulls out a pistol and waves it at us. "I should have drilled both of you and left you to rot in that mine!"

Daphne clutches my arm.

The older man reaches out and pushes Mr. C.'s arm down. "Put that away, Findlay. You're just lucky I was standing down here or we'd be on our way to a prison cell!"

Mr. Carhartt—Findlay—grumbles. "I had it under control."

The older man doesn't bother replying to that.

"I told him we already called the sheriff," I say. "They'll be here any minute."

The older man sucks in a deep breath. "I very much doubt that. But if you start behaving and quit telling lies, you might just have a chance to survive this unfortunate encounter."

"You're Mr. Big, aren't you?" Daphne asks.

Despite the seriousness of the situation, the man chuckles. "Mr. Big? Where did you get that? From a James Bond movie?"

"You're the one who hired Findlay. The one we heard him talking to on the phone?"

Mr. Big gives Findlay an exasperated look that says, *How did I hire an idiot like you?* Then, he turns back to Daphne and me. "That's none of your business."

"Are you behind all of the recent thefts of Charlie Russell's work?"

If we weren't in deep trouble before, we are now. Mr. Big narrows his eyes and his forehead wrinkles up like an accordion.

Daphne, I think, *Don't you ever keep your mouth shut?*

"What do you know about Russell?" Mr. Big says.

Daphne starts to answer, but I cut her off. "Nothing. Only that he's famous and is really good at painting cowboys and buffaloes."

Mr. Big doesn't buy it. "You know about the other thefts, too?"

Daphne doesn't answer, but throws me a guilty glance.

Oh, well, I think. *The game is up now.*

"Why are you doing it?" I ask. "Russell's work is part of our national heritage. What right do you have to steal it for yourself?"

"What right?" the man hisses. "I have *every* right. Some of Russell's best paintings should have been passed on to *me.*"

Daphne and I glance at each other. I am thinking, *Is this guy nuts?* I am also thinking that it may be good to keep him talking now.

"Uh, how is that?" I venture.

"That hooligan Thomas Gilcrease stole them right out from under my family's noses."

"Gilcrease..." Daphne says. "You're not talking about the same guy who started the Gilcrease Museum in Oklahoma, are you?"

I also remember Agent Bullock mentioning the attempted theft there.

"That is exactly who I am talking about!" Mr. Big thunders. "My uncle, Philip Gillette Cole, spent years amassing the greatest collection of Western art anywhere."

"You mean your great-great uncle," Findlay corrects him.

Mr. Big glares at him. "Yes, my *great-great* uncle. Now keep your pie hole shut!

"Anyway, when other collectors looked down their noses at Western art, my great-great uncle filled his mansion with hundreds of paintings and sculptures by the country's greatest artists—Russell, Remington, N.C. Wyeth."

"So?" I ask.

"After my Uncle Cole died, the collection should have been passed to his relatives. Instead, that snake Thomas Gilcrease bought the entire collection for less than you could buy a single Russell painting for today!"

"Hm." Daphne presses down the tip of her nose with her finger. "I'm trying to understand this. Are you telling us that because your great-great-great-great-great uncle—"

"*Great-great,*" hisses Mr. Big.

"Oh, right. But you're telling us that because Philip Cole didn't leave some of his collection to, what, your third cousin twice removed? That because of this, you have the right to steal Charlie Russell's art for yourself?"

"What I'm saying is that my *great grandmother* was robbed of her rightful inheritance, and I'm only trying to get back part of what's mine."

"But," I say, "the Russells that Philip Cole collected are all in the Gilcrease Museum, aren't they? The paintings *you're* stealing never even belonged to Cole in the first place."

Mr. Big scoffs. "A minor point."

"No it's not," says Daphne. "If I used that kind of thinking, I could go out and find an excuse to take almost anything!"

Mr. Big glares at Daphne. "What do you know? You're just a kid."

I defend her. "She knows enough not to steal something that isn't hers."

Daphne flashes me a smile.

Findlay steps forward. "Enough of this, Mr. Paxton."

Mr. Big wheels on him. "I told you not to use my name!"

But Findlay shows some spine. "As if it matters

now! We've got to figure out what to do with these two brats until it's safe to get out of here."

"You'd better leave now," I tell them. "I think I hear sirens coming."

Mr. Big—aka Mr. Paxton—gives me an annoyed look. "Oh do be quiet, will you?"

Then, he turns to Findlay. "I need to go get our vehicle. I had to hide it a couple miles away to make sure no one would notice it, but I'll be back in less than an hour. By then, most of the tourists ought to be gone and it should be safer to move out of here."

"What am I supposed to do while you're out on your little hike?" Findlay asks.

"Stay hidden outside the building and keep watch for anyone coming."

Findlay nods to us. "And them?"

Mr. Paxton draws his lips back into an ugly smile. "Throw them in a vat."

Twenty-Nine

"**N**ow what?" Daphne asks.

I place both hands against the side of the circular, thick-walled redwood vat once used to separate gold from crushed up ore. I push hard against the tight-fitting planks. Then, I step back and give the boards my best Jackie Chan front kick. Instead of shattering the planks with my super-human strength, I bounce back in a heap on the dusty, bird-poop-splattered floor.

I glance up at Daphne, who looks down at me, trying to smother a smile.

"It was a nice try."

I cough and stand up. "We need some kind of tool to pry between the boards."

We both search the vat but can't find a thing.

"Do you have any tools?" I ask.

Mr. Carhartt—Findlay—heaved our backpacks into the sagebrush outside the mill, but Daphne makes a show of patting her pockets. "I usually carry my chainsaw with me, but I must have left it back in camp." Then, she says, "Boost me up."

Duh, I tell myself. *I should have thought of that.*

The walls of the vat are maybe nine, ten feet high. I am not sure that I can get Daphne up to the top, but it's worth a try. I step over to the side of the vat.

"How do you want to do this?" Daphne asks.

I pick the scab of an old zit on my cheek. "Good question. Here."

I lean my back against the vat wall and lock my hands into a stirrup in front of me. "Step up onto my shoulders."

Daphne comes face to face with me. Instead of stepping into my hands, however, she does something different. *Very* different. She leans forward and presses her lips softly against mine.

This time, our lips don't just twitch against each other. They seem to know exactly what to do. In fact, they spend quite a few seconds knowing what to do before Daphne pulls away again, smiling shyly at me.

Her peach shampoo scent swims through my nasal passages. My lips feel like they've just gone to heaven without me. Every nerve in my body leaps up and down shouting "Whoo-hoo! Hot Dang! That's what I'm talkin' about!"

But the fact is that I'm speechless.

"I'm sorry I messed up our first kiss before," Daphne apologizes.

"Uh..."

"You just caught me by surprise. That's all."

Finally, I swallow, and find some words. "I thought you were mad at me. That you didn't want me to kiss you."

She blushes—one of the few times I've ever seen her do that. She tucks some hair behind her ear. "No. I've been thinking about kissing you ever since before we first held hands."

"You *have*? I thought I was the only one."

She shakes her head and her green eyes seem to be on fire. "I just didn't know how. Or maybe I thought it would mess things up between us." Then, she looks more serious. "It didn't, did it?"

I grin. "Are you kidding?"

She also smiles. "Good."

"In fact," I tell her. "I think we should do it again."

I lean toward her, but feel her hand press firmly against my chest. "Easy, killer. Maybe after we get out of here."

That snaps me back to reality, and I look around at our circular prison. "Oh, yeah."

I again lock my hands into a stirrup and boost Daphne up onto my shoulders. Then, grunting, I straighten up with my back against the wall.

"Don't wobble so much," I say, trying to hold her feet steady. "Can you reach?"

"No. Are you strong enough to hold my feet in your hands and straighten your arms up?"

Am I strong enough? I think sourly. *I'll show you.*

But when I straighten my arms up and Daphne steps up into my hands, my whole body almost buckles.

"Can you reach now?" I gasp, trying not to let her know the pain I'm in.

Suddenly, I hear a loud SMACK above me and Daphne tumbles back down onto the vat floor.

Findlay's angry voice shouts, "What the heck are you kids doing?"

I squat down next to Daphne. "Are you alright?"

Daphne rubs her knee and her face is furious. With effort she stands up and yells. "Why did you do that? I could have broken my neck!"

"You try that again and I'll break it for you!" Findlay yells back.

Daphne leans down and picks up a handful of dirt and bird droppings and hurls it over the side of the vat.

"Hey!" Findlay yells as poop and dirt rain down on him. "You little brat!"

"You'd better not have children!" Daphne shouts at him. "You'd be a terrible father!"

"Don't worry! If anything would keep me from having kids, it's you two! I'm just right outside. You try to escape again, and I'll make sure you're stuck in there forever. You hear me?"

Neither Daphne nor I answer, and Findlay's footsteps stalk away.

"What did he do to you?" I ask.

"He tried to whack my fingers with a stick! What a jerk! What a moron!"

I don't think I've ever seen Daphne this mad before—except for maybe that time I made fun of the vampire romance books she was reading. It's a solid reminder to stay on her good side.

Daphne starts pacing the vat, and I see that she's limping.

"Geez, you're really hurt." Now, I'm getting mad, too, and find myself imagining putting both Findlay and Mr. Big—Mr. Paxton—through a crushing machine and separating *them* for their ore content.

"I'm alright," Daphne mutters. "I just hit my kneecap when I fell."

From inside the vat, it's hard to tell what time it is, but through some gaps in the roof, I can see that the sun has definitely moved on toward late afternoon.

"We've been in here a while. Do you think our moms are worried about us yet?" I ask.

"Probably," Daphne says, still limping around the vat, looking for a way out. "If only they'd left us something to stand on—anything!"

She looks at me and says, "I could try boosting you up there."

Remembering how my arms almost buckled, I shake my head. "Uh, it's harder than you might think."

Daphne glares at me. "Slate Stephens, are you calling me weak?"

"Uh, no. It's just that..."

But Daphne relaxes her glare. "You're probably right. I don't think I could hold you. It's too bad they don't have telephones in here."

And suddenly, I feel my heart leap. "Daphne!"

She looks at me. "What?"

I reach into my pocket.

Thirty

"**W**hy didn't you tell me you had the radio?"

I shrug, embarrassed. "I forgot. Besides, I don't know how far it will reach from in here. This building might totally block the signal."

"Well, quick, try it. Paxson will be back with the car any second!"

I turn on the radio and press the transmit button. "Dad, Len, answer. This is Slate. Dad, Len, answer your radio *now*!"

I release the button and whisper. "Do you hear anyone coming?"

Daphne shakes her head. "Not yet."

I wait a few seconds, then try again. "Dad, Len. Please answer your radio. It's an emergency. Come in, Dad and Len."

Again, nothing.

"I don't think the signal's getting out of here," I say.

Daphne studies the walls of our circular jail cell. "You might be right. Especially if they're all the way up near Road Agents Rock."

Suddenly, the radio crackles. "SATE!"

"Lily!" I shout into the radio. "Lily, where are you?"

"At the picnic table."

"Which picnic table? In our campsite?"

Daphne and I look at each other excitedly.

"What's a campset?"

"Never mind! Put Mom or Theresa on the radio."

"They're not here."

"Where are they?"

"T'resa is looking for you. Mommy's in the bathroom."

"You mean the outhouse?"

"Yeah."

Daphne tugs on my arm and hisses, "Slate, I think they're coming!"

Beads of sweat pop out on my forehead.

"Lily! This is important! You have to give a message to Mom and Theresa."

"What message?"

"Tell them that we are trapped over at the Bannack Mill. Do you have that?"

"The Bannack Milk."

"No, the Bannack *Mill*."

"What's a mill?"

"Never mind that. Just tell them that the bad guys have caught us and to call the police."

"Okay."

"Tell it back to me."

But before Lily can respond, Findlay's head appears above us. "HEY! WHAT DO YOU THINK YOU'RE DOING?"

I turn off the radio and shove it into my pocket,

but it's too late. Findlay lowers a dusty wooden ladder into the vat and orders us to get out.

Once we're outside, Findlay holds out his hand. "Give it to me."

"Give you what?"

Findlay steps closer. "Quit playing games."

"Okay, okay." I reach into my pocket and hand him the radio. Findlay looks at it and then spins and throws it against the wall of the vat. The radio shatters into a dozen pieces.

"What was that?" Mr. Paxson marches into the building.

"The kids had a radio," Findlay fumes.

"And you just destroyed it?"

"Well, yeah."

"You imbecile. We could have listened in on what their parents or whoever were doing."

Findlay's angry eyes cool down with that little bit of insight.

"Who did they call?" Paxson demands.

Findlay turns to me. "Who did you call?"

"The police."

Findlay grabs me by the shirt and his Jolly Rancher breath hits me like a watermelon patch. "It *wasn't* the police. Quit fooling with me kid, or I swear—"

"Never mind!" Paxson interrupts. "It doesn't matter. I've got the car. You get the paintings and bring them outside."

Findlay is still clutching my shirt. "What about these two?"

Mr. Paxson narrows his eyes first at me, then at Daphne.

"Bring 'em along."

As Paxson leaves, Findlay drags me roughly over to another vat.

"Hey, leave him alone!" Daphne shouts, sounding a lot braver than I know she feels.

Findlay doesn't respond, but he does let go of me. He reaches under the vat next to the thick supporting beams that it stands on, and pulls out two more plastic bags.

"Are those the Russells?" I ask him.

"These are them," Findlay mumbles. "You carry one. You—" He points to Daphne. "You take the other one."

"Can we look at them?"

Findlay glares at me. "No, you can't look at them. Hurry up."

Daphne and I each pick up a painting, and Findlay shoves us toward the opening in the building.

"Not so rough," I protest. "I might drop the painting."

"You know, there's no reason for you to take us," Daphne says.

Findlay doesn't answer.

"Kidnapping charges are a lot more serious than theft. Why don't you just throw us back in the vat, and you can make a clean getaway?"

"Hmph! I thought you called the police?" Findlay gruffs.

"Well, um, yeah. But you still have time. They have to drive here all the way from Dillon."

Findlay gives us each another shove. "Just keep movin'."

We approach a big black extended-cab pickup truck with a rental car sticker on the back windshield. Mr. Paxson is standing next to the open driver's side door.

Daphne looks up at the late afternoon sky and tells Mr. Paxson, "You know on a day like today, a convertible would have been a lot more comfortable."

"Get in the back seat," Paxson growls.

The pickup has one of those narrow backseats that make adults scrunch up their legs so that their kneecaps bump against their front teeth. For Daphne and me, it's not so bad—except for the fact that we're getting into a car with two criminals who just might not have our health and safety as their first priority.

I hesitate before climbing in. "It's a lot harder to travel with hostages. You don't really need us anymore."

Paxson glares. "Don't worry. For you, this is going to be a short trip."

Reluctantly, I crawl in next to Daphne and they slide the paintings in between our knees and the seat.

Paxson takes the driver's seat and puts the truck in gear even before Findlay has jumped into the front passenger side. Then, spitting gravel, the truck lurches forward.

Thirty-One

We drive along the bypass road until it 'T's into the main Bannack gravel access road. If we turn right, it will lead us into the Bannack visitor's parking lot. The truck, though, turns left on a course that will take us right by our campground on the way to the highway.

Findlay turns and shoves his pistol in our faces. "Keep your heads down and do not even think about yelling out the window, got it?"

Daphne and I both nod, but before I lower my head I catch a glimpse of Lily down below the road in our campsite.

My heart pounds, and I think, *Please Lily! Get the message straight!*

Even with my naturally optimistic nature, I have to admit it's a longshot. Lily's not even four, after all. How many three-year-olds would transmit a message like that correctly?

I feel Daphne's hand reach for mine. With my head down it's hard to see her face, but I lock my fingers in hers and squeeze.

After a few seconds, Daphne asks, "Can we put our heads back up? I feel like a flamingo."

"For now," Findlay tells us. "But if we see another

car, you get those heads down pronto, you hear me?"

When I raise my head, I see Grasshopper Creek out the window.

"Look," I tell Daphne, pointing to a large pool at a dogleg bend in the creek. "I think that's Dorothy's Hole."

"The place where that girl drowned?"

"Yeah."

"What are you talking about?" Mr. Paxson demands.

"There's a ghost in Bannack," I explain. "Of a teenaged girl who drowned in Grasshopper Creek a long time ago."

Paxson slows for a stop sign, then turns the truck right, onto a paved road that will take us out to Highway 271. "Rubbish," he says about Dorothy's ghost, but Findlay asks, "Where's this ghost hang out?"

I shrug. "Not sure, except she's definitely been seen in the schoolhouse."

Now, Findlay's eyes widen. "Hey, I think I saw that girl!"

Paxson's head swivels in his direction. "Who? The ghost?"

Findlay nods. "That's right. I was scoping out the town, trying to figure out where to stash the Russell paintings, and I saw this girl in an old-time dress walking by herself down the street."

"You *did*?" Daphne asks.

Findlay lowers his pistol. "Yep. I was going to call to her, but she seemed lost in her own world. There was something very creepy about her—like maybe she'd escaped from a mental institution."

"Oh, for Pete's sake!" Paxson exclaims. "I'm beginning to think *you* escaped from a mental institution. You didn't see any ghost. It was probably just a tourist wandering around. And what were you thinking, considering calling out to her?"

"I'll bet it *was* Dorothy," I tell Findlay, trying to widen the rift between him and Paxson.

"Where's she buried?" Findlay asks us.

"I don't—"

Before I can finish my sentence, all of us hear the distant sounds of sirens.

"Dang it!" Paxson hollers. "How'd they get here so fast?"

"They probably already had some cars in the area," Findlay tells him.

The road doesn't give us a view of what's up ahead, but as the sirens grow louder, it's pretty clear they are coming toward us. Daphne and I look at each other with open mouths, barely able to contain our glee.

"We're trapped!" Paxson yells. "I'm going to turn around."

"No!" Findlay tells him. "Up here, past that graveyard, turn right. We can get out that way before they spot us."

Paxson slows. "You sure about this?"

"Yeah," Findlay tells him. "This road leads up to a bunch of other dirt roads. If we can make it up there, they'll never find us."

In the rearview mirror, I can see Paxson scowl. "You'd better be right about this, Findlay."

As the truck roars past the cemetery, I also happen to glance at the fence surrounding the graveyard, and the old tombstones inside of it, and something flashes through my mind. It's just a brief image, like what you see in the flicker of a strobe light. Before I can process it, however, Paxson brakes hard and swings right, onto the same dirt road we followed with our dads a couple of days earlier.

Daphne turns to me and mouths the words "Road Agents Rock".

I nod.

The truck bounces along the road, and then begins climbing a steep, sage-covered hillside.

Suddenly, we can all see the flashing lights of three patrol cars speeding down the paved access road toward Bannack. They are still about half a mile from the cemetery, but are closing fast.

"Do you think they see us?" Findlay asks.

Paxson glances down below as he continues to drive. "We'd better hope not. They were still pretty far away when we turned off."

Findlay glances behind the truck. "We're not kicking

up any dust, either, thanks to the rains yesterday."

Daphne and I also look behind the truck and see that, unfortunately, Findlay is correct. Still, I'm hoping that the patrol cars will spot us up on the hillside above them, and I eagerly watch as they approach the cemetery turnoff.

Daphne and I again squeeze hands, waiting to see if the cars will turn in pursuit.

Then, Findlay yelps. "Yahoo! The cops zipped right past the cemetery! We're home free!"

Paxson smacks the steering wheel in celebration, then grins at us in the rearview mirror. "Looks like you're stuck with us now, kids."

I watch Daphne's face sag and her eyes start to shimmer.

I grasp her hand harder and mouth to her, "It will be okay," but I'm not sure either of us believes that now.

Thirty-Two

We continue up the dirt road. The sun is starting to set, and its brilliant light saturates the hills and mountains with a rich yellow color. I'd enjoy it if Daphne and I weren't in the company of two art-crazed psychopathic megalomaniacs.

"So, what's the plan?" Findlay asks.

Mr. Paxson lets out a big sigh and loosens his grip on the steering wheel. "Easy. You guide us out of here. We link up with the Interstate, then head down to Pocatello to catch a plane."

"Not until you pay me we don't," Findlay informs him. "You bring the money?"

"Don't you worry about that."

Findlay's eyes narrow and he points his gun at Paxson. "Don't give me that, Paxson. I'll ask you again, you bring the money?"

With Findlay's gun pointing at him, Paxon's arrogance deflates. "R-relax. Relax. The cash is under the seat."

Findlay glares at him. "It better be."

We keep driving. The road grows steeper and more rutted. Then suddenly, on one uphill stretch, the truck's back wheels start to spin.

"What the—?" Paxson exclaims.

"It's the road," Findlay tells him. "It's still wet from last night's rains."

"It's called gumbo," I chime in. "When it gets wet, it turns really slippery."

"I don't care what it's called," Paxson says. "How do we get out of it?"

"Put it in four-wheel drive," Findlay says.

"We don't have four-wheel drive, Numbskull!"

Now, it's Findlay's turn to get mad. "What? Didn't I tell you to rent a four-wheel drive truck?"

"It cost $200 more. I didn't think we'd need it."

"I swear," Findlay says, looking back at Daphne and me. "Why is it that rich people are the biggest cheapskates on earth?"

Daphne and I shrug, but it doesn't help the truck move any faster. Our tires keep spinning, and we slow to a crawl.

Again, my hopes rise that we can somehow get away. Daphne's smile tells me she is thinking the same thing.

We continue to slide and lurch up the rutted road. Once or twice, we get stuck, and Paxson has to roll the truck backward onto a flatter stretch of road so that we can build up enough speed to climb a rise or make it over a bump. Finally, after about two miles, we link up with the original stage road leading out of Bannack. Unfortunately for Daphne and me, the road here gets a little drier and easier, and our captors again relax.

Findlay glances back at us. "So, what about them?"

"I've been thinking about that," Paxson says. Speaking directly to us, he says, "I'd like to let you kids go, but I think you know just a little too much about us now."

"We don't!" Daphne insists. "We don't even know your real names."

"Or where you live or even your favorite kind of breakfast cereal," I add.

Daphne shoots me a 'shut up' look, then says to the crooks, "Besides, we promise we won't tell anything about you. We'll just say that you blindfolded us the entire time."

Paxson studies us in the rearview mirror. "I appreciate that, kids. Really, I do." Then, he makes a little clucking sound with his tongue. "The thing is, I trust you two just fine. It's the police I don't trust. They have a way of getting things out of even the most well-meaning witnesses."

"They won't get anything from us," I insist. "Even the FBI hardly knows anything about you."

Findlay's head snaps back toward us.

"Did you say the FBI? You've talked to the FBI?"

"No!" Daphne quickly says. "He just means that we haven't heard anything from them."

Paxson exchanges a look with Findlay, and says, "Well, we'll see."

Findlay unwraps another Jolly Rancher, and tells Paxson, "There are a lot of abandoned mines between here and the highway."

Paxson doesn't reply, but when I try to swallow, I discover that my mucus membranes have suddenly gone on strike.

"Why don't you just let us out here or up at Road Agents Rock?" Daphne asks. "By the time we walk back to Bannack, you'll be long gone."

The two men remain silent and, in desperation, I glance at our two passenger doors to see if they're locked. They are, and besides, Paxson probably has the hidden child safety locks on, too. I also think about trying to kick out the truck's back window, but am not at all sure it'll break. Even if it does, Findlay could easily grab us or shoot us before we get clear.

I glance down at the garbage bags holding the Russell masterpieces and think, *What if I found something sharp and threatened to tear up the paintings if they don't release us?*

Another dumb plan. It wouldn't work for one thing. For another, I don't think I could ever bring myself to damage a Russell original.

I look over at Daphne and use a shrug and facial expressions to ask her if she has any ideas.

She looks as scared as I feel, and shakes her head.

"There's Road Agents Rock," Findlay tells Paxson. "What's the story on that?"

"It's where the bad guys used to rob the stage

coaches coming out of Bannack," Findlay explains.

Paxson laughs. "Too bad we weren't around then. We could have had some serious fun robbing—"

Before Paxson can finish his sentence, three of the truck's four tires suddenly explode and the truck swerves into a huge thicket of sagebrush.

"What the—?" Findlay exclaims.

Half a dozen armed men dressed in camouflage swoop down on us.

"OUT OF THE TRUCK!" they yell, rifles pointed at Findlay and Paxson.

Findlay starts to raise his gun, but his window shatters and he is forcibly dragged through it and thrown to the ground. At the same time, our doors fly open and strong hands grab Daphne and me and carry us in opposite directions away from the truck.

There is more shouting, but no more loud explosions. From the safety of Road Agents Rock, I watch to see armed police and sheriff's deputies in bulletproof vests handcuff Paxson and Findlay and hustle them into a waiting four-wheel drive vehicle. Seconds later, the vehicle is tearing down the road toward Bannack.

When it's all clear, the police officer who rescued me walks me back to the truck, where I find Daphne already talking to Agent Bullock. Daphne throws her arms around me.

"Slate," she whispers in my ear. "I thought we were—"

"Me, too."

We separate, but keep gripping each other's hands. I ask Agent Bullock. "How did you know where we were?"

He's still wearing his dark glasses. "We didn't for sure. But your mom called from the Bannack park headquarters with the message from Lela."

"You mean Lily?" I ask, smiling at Daphne.

"That's right. Your sister. We looked at a map and realized that unless they wanted to walk, there were only two ways out of Bannack. If we didn't intercept you along the main road down there, we'd catch you here. The thing is, we didn't know if we'd get here in time to set up the ambush."

"That's because of the gumbo," I tell him. "It slowed us down coming up the hill."

"Well, thank our lucky stars for that," Agent Bullock says.

Just then, the Beaverhead County Sheriff steps forward. "I was hopin' that gumbo might still have some slickness to it," he tells us. "We figured Road Agents Rock was as good a place as any for an ambush. Heck, if the stage robbers could use it, why couldn't we? So we set up marksmen from our joint tactical squad on this side of the road. As soon as your vehicle slowed, we shot out the tires."

Daphne and I look at each other, alarmed.

"You *shot* out the tires? *With guns?*" Daphne asks, appalled. "I thought you put spikes in the road."

"Don't worry," the sheriff assures us. "We only brought our best shooters."

I'm not sure if we should be terrified or relieved by that remark.

"Do our parents know we're safe?" Daphne suddenly asks.

"We radioed them as soon as you were out of the truck," Agent Bullock assures us. "In fact, I'll give you a ride down to them right now. Then, you're going to have to come into Dillon to answer some questions."

Agent Bullock begins to turn away, but I say, "Can we see the Russell paintings first?"

Bullock looks at the sheriff, who shrugs.

"I don't see why not."

The sheriff leads us over to the bed of the pickup truck and tells Rick, our favorite sheriff's deputy, "Take them out for a minute."

Rick removes *Bronc to Breakfast* first. As we did when seeing it on the computer a few days earlier, Daphne and I both laugh. The painting is hilarious, with the horse kicking its way through the campfire. I am amazed by how much life Russell has put into the action.

Next, Rick pulls out *The Fireboat.*

"Nice timing," Agent Bullock notes, and indeed it is. Behind us, the real sun just happens to be sinking over the mountains. It mimics the last rays of light on Russell's three Indian horsemen as they watch the steamboat making its way up the Missouri River.

"Wow," I say, awed by the painting. In person, the colors and texture are a hundred times richer than they are from a book or website. And even though the painting's subject saddens me, I am relieved that this masterpiece will remain in the public for all to appreciate.

After a minute, Agent Bullock asks, "You ready?"

Daphne and I both nod. Then, we climb into his vehicle and head back down the hill.

Thirty-Three

For the second time this summer, Daphne and I are sucked into a media maelstrom. After being debriefed by the sheriff, police, and FBI, we get at least a dozen interview requests from newspaper, television, and radio reporters. We also receive thirty different requests to write guest blogs on the Web. I let Daphne, the Internet Queen, deal with those.

Lily gets even more attention than we do, and handles reporters' questions like an old pro. When one reporter asks her how she knew how to work the radio, she answers, "It's easy. I can show you." When asked if she was scared when she gave my radio message to Mom, she answers, "No. I was hungry."

All in all, the Russell heist story seems even bigger than when we found Cat, the governor's dog. It doesn't hurt that the paintings were recovered near Bannack, a place known for its vigilantes, or that they were worth several million dollars. But reporters seem especially interested in the fact that Daphne and I ended up solving both this crime and the governor's dog disappearance.

"Are you going to start your own detective

agency?" Nick Spotley from the Rocky Mountain News Agency asks us.

"No," Daphne tells him, sweeping a strand of black hair behind her ear. "We've got school and our parents will kill us if we don't get our homework finished."

Nick laughs, but uses the quote to wrap up his piece, which runs in newspapers all across the West.

But Daphne wasn't joking about school and, in fact, the end of the summer is very much on our minds. After the ambush at Road Agents Rock, my mom and Theresa try to whisk us back home to Missoula so we can shop for school clothes and all of that other boring stuff.

"No!" Daphne and I both shout.

"We want to stay here in Bannack," Daphne explains.

"At least for a few more days," I plead.

The Parental Units all look at each other, mystified.

"Why?" Mom finally asks.

"Uh..." None of the parents know that Daphne and I still have unfinished business in Bannack.

As usual, Daphne saves me. "We haven't even had a chance to go fishing in Grasshopper Creek," she says. "Besides, we got several blog requests to write about Bannack. We have to do some more research before we go back."

I am not sure any of the parents swallow this,

but none of them seem willing or able to mount a rebuttal.

"Well, I guess it's okay," Len says.

Dad shrugs. "Yeah. It's nice to have serfs around to cook and clean up for us."

Normally, I would challenge that remark, but I let it pass.

With a last glance at each other, Mom and Theresa consent and it's all settled. Daphne and I get four more days to find the missing vigilantes' treasure.

As it turns out, we don't need that long.

The next morning, after the dads head off to find their own gold, Daphne and I sit at the camp picnic table. Like a lizard, I feel the sun slowly raise my body temperature up to operational range, but after the recent storm, I can feel an extra chill in the air. Fall is definitely on its way.

Daphne feels the chill, too, and scoots over next to me to get warm. I put my arm around her waist and momentarily forget all about the treasure. Daphne gets me back on track.

"So," she says. "Where are we?"

Reluctantly removing my arm from her waist, I spread out the note we found at the schoolhouse. For the thousandth time, we read through the entire list of clues:

From the place of Plummer's demise,
Walk to town to seek your prize.

A yellow journal points you to
The location of your second clue.

If your thoughts fall into line,
You'll recognize Our Dear Lord's prime.

To a House Divided, take this mark,
And count to how a wolf is cloaked.

And with that precious knowledge stored,
Find the dwelling of one once adored.

Of its bricks take proper stock,
And pace them down a Confederate walk.

A lucky one will dig with pleasure,
To claim the vigilantes' treasure.

Daphne traces her finger down to the fourth stanza. "So," she says. "We agree that how the wolf is cloaked means a sheep, right?"

"Right."

"The question is, who was the person that was once adored? You said you think it was Henry Plummer, but I don't think that sounds right."

And that's when it comes back to me. That strange flash I had in the truck when Daphne and I were being kidnapped.

"It's not," I tell Daphne.

She shoves her shoulder against mine. "It's not what?"

"It's not Plummer."

Daphne leans back to look at me. "Well, who is it then?"

"I'm not sure. But I think I have an idea. Grab the camp shovel."

Thirty-Four

Ilead Daphne out of the campground, but instead of heading toward the ghost town, we turn left onto the road out of Bannack, Daphne swinging the camp shovel like a pendulum as we walk.

"Where are we going?"

"You'll see."

Twenty minutes later, we reach the "new" Bannack cemetery.

"Here?" Daphne asks in a slightly whiney voice. "You made me walk to a cemetery? Why?"

"When we were in that truck with Paxson and Findlay, I thought I saw something."

"What?"

"I'll show you." I pull open the creaky gate to the graveyard and we enter.

The cemetery covers maybe half an acre. I've never been inside before, but when I first arrived in Bannack, I visited the original graveyard up on the hill above town. Like the old one, this new cemetery is full of grass and sagebrush and prickly pear cactuses that have reclaimed the land over the last century. At both cemeteries, people built little wooden picket fences around many of the gravesites, perhaps to keep coyotes and other varmints from digging into the graves. Many of these fences have fallen apart over time, but here, many more of the original headstones remain.

"Look," Daphne points as we begin walking past graves. "That grave marker is wooden."

"I guess people couldn't afford real stone back then."

"Look how young these people were when they died."

I nod. Doing quick mental calculations on the dates inscribed in the grave markers, I see that many of the people buried here died in their twenties and teens. A lot were children.

"Life must have been hard," I tell Daphne.

"I'm glad I'm alive now and not then. Where are we going, anyway?"

"Over here," I say, just as a big maroon town car pulls into the parking lot outside the fence. I ignore it and lead Daphne through the sagebrush to the southern end of cemetery.

"Look."

Daphne's mouth opens and her green eyes dance. "Slate!" she exclaims.

In front of us stands a white marble headstone. That's not the exciting part. What's exciting is that on the top of the headstone sits a little carved lamb.

"Do you think this is it?" I ask Daphne.

She gives my shoulder an enthusiastic shove. "It's got to be! That is, unless there are others like it. How did you know it was here?"

"By accident. When Paxson and Findlay drove us by here, I was looking out the window and caught a glimpse of it. Really, I wasn't even sure what I'd seen, but I knew it was something important."

I read the name on the stone. "Velma George. Born January 5th, 1907. Died October 25th, 1909."

"Slate, she was less than three years old." Daphne's voice is sad, and I feel a lump in my own throat.

"Maybe they carved sheep only for very young children."

"Get the clues out."

I pull out the sheet of paper again, and still clutching the shovel, Daphne steps up next to me. We both read.

"Well," I say. "A child would definitely be someone 'once adored', wouldn't she?"

Daphne agrees. "But it's a little vague. I mean, why would they refer to just any child? Would you write a clue like that?"

"No, not really."

Then, she points to the next line. "And what's this line? *Of its bricks take proper stock, and pace them down a Confederate walk?*"

I circle the gravestone and feel my pulse quicken. "Look here!"

Daphne hurries around behind the marker. In the back, we both see that the marble has been chiseled out to look like bricks. I quickly count them up.

"There are thirteen of them," I say excitedly. "That's got to be a clue. Maybe they mean thirteen feet from this spot?"

"No, it's probably paces," Daphne says.

"Yeah!" We are both talking rapidly now.

"But which direction?" Daphne looks all around us and then back at the words 'Confederate Walk'."

"South!" we both blurt at the same time.

I stand next to the grave and glance up at the sun to get my bearing. Then, with large strides, I pace off thirteen steps and stop to find I am standing in the middle of what looks like a rabbit trail.

"Now what?" I ask. "Do you think they meant to dig *here*?"

I hear voices behind me and see that two people are walking slowly through the cemetery. They must be the people who drove up in the town car.

Daphne lowers her voice. "This doesn't seem like the right spot. Even if your paces weren't the right length… What about that gravesite there?"

Daphne drops the shovel where I was standing, and we both walk a few yards to a gravesite that looks better kept than any of the others. The headstone reads "Mabel Ovitt."

"Hey," I say. "That's the woman who ran herself over with the car. The last person to actually live in Bannack."

"You're right," Daphne says. "She was definitely

someone who was 'once adored', don't you think?"

I am confused now. I look from the clues in my hand to the grave marker and back again. "Yeah, but see, she didn't die until 1968. How could that have anything to do with the vigilantes' gold?"

"Maybe it's just a coincidence that Mabel is buried here," Daphne says. "Maybe the clues are just referring to the child's headstone."

I pause and pull thoughtfully on my eyebrows.

Daphne pokes me. "What is it?"

"Well," I tell her. "There's something else that's bothering me."

"What?"

"It's just..."

"It's just *what*?"

"It's just all too easy. I mean, we hardly know anything about Bannack and we were able to figure this out."

"Do you think we misread the clues?"

"No. I think we read them correctly. But something...something's not right."

Daphne sighs and nods. "I know what you mean. I've had the same feeling. I just didn't want to admit it to myself."

Then, we hear a voice behind us.

"Did you know Mabel?"

Thirty-Five

Daphne and I whirl around to see a slightly stooped, gray-haired woman dressed in a purple floral print dress. I don't know how I didn't hear her walk up behind us. *Those old people can be mighty sneaky!* I think.

"Mabel was a good friend of mine," the woman continues. "Are you related to her somehow?"

"You lived in Bannack?" I ask. Beyond her, I see a younger man, perhaps her son, examining some gravesites about fifty yards away.

"Oh, yes," the older woman answers, smiling and stepping closer. "I was one of the last kids to attend the Bannack School."

"You're kidding!"

Daphne and I gape at each other.

"What was that like?" Daphne asks, voice straining with curiosity.

"Oh, it was wonderful," the woman says. Then, she laughs. "At least it was wonderful some of the time. When it got down to twenty or thirty below zero, that could certainly put a chill on your day. But it seems to me all us kids were happy here."

"Why did you leave?"

"We didn't have any choice, dear. The mine and

the mill closed again and there got to be too few students to keep the school open. That's when my parents decided it was time to head on up to Butte."

"That must have stunk," I say.

The woman laughs, but then explains, "I suppose we were all sad at first. But the big city offered us a lot of opportunities we didn't have out here. Why, I remember one time when we'd just arrived in—"

The woman stops and looks at the piece of paper I am holding. "Say, what have you got there?"

"Uh." I also look at the paper in my hand and then over at Daphne.

She shrugs. "We might as well show it to her, Slate. We're not going to start digging up the cemetery, are we?"

Normally, I would object, but my uneasiness about the clues makes me relent.

I sigh and hand over the note to the old woman.

I notice for the first time that she has some kind of condition that makes her body tremble. Her hand shakes slightly as she holds the note, but she reads it slowly and with interest. Finally, she looks up at me. "Where on earth did you find this?"

"Uh, it was jammed under one of the seats in the schoolhouse."

To our surprise, the woman breaks into a dentured grin. "Well, I'll be…"

"What?" I ask. "Do you think it's real?"

The woman chuckles. "Oh, it's real alright—at least for what it is."

Daphne steps closer. "What do you mean?"

The woman holds up the note. "I remember this clearly."

"You've seen it before?" I ask.

"Yes, indeed," she says. "After Mabel died, we all held a reunion here in Bannack. Everyone who had attended school came back for a weekend of camping and festivities. Someone put together a contest. If you solved all of the clues on this sheet, you got a prize."

Daphne rolls her eyes. "Well, *that* explains a lot."

"What was the prize?" I ask.

The woman pinches her chin in thought. "Why, I can't even remember now, isn't that funny? I never was good at figuring out things like this. We worked in teams, but another team solved the riddles first."

"Well, are we in the right place? Did we follow the clues correctly?"

The woman slowly spins around, then says, "Almost. Follow me."

We traipse across the cemetery to the northeast corner, where we find an almost identical tombstone with a lamb on top of it. On this marker, though, the head of the lamb is missing. I read the name on the stone and see that it is for another baby.

"Perry J. Meade," Daphne reads. "Born February 26th, 1895. Died September 14th, 1896."

"I believe that this here is where the clues led," the woman explains. "See, over there is where Dorothy is buried."

We look over to a fenced-in gravesite without any kind of headstone.

"You mean the Dorothy who drowned? Is that where we were supposed to dig?" I ask.

"Oh, heavens no. What do the clues tell you to do?"

"Walk thirteen paces south," Daphne says.

"Well, let's do that." With surprising strength, the woman counts out thirteen steps in the right direction—and adds a couple more for good measure.

"Here," she says.

We look to our left to see a slightly sunken area of sagebrush-covered dirt. "I'm pretty sure this is where they buried the silver dollars."

Daphne and I look at each other. "Silver dollars?"

A pleased expression brightens the woman's face. "That's right! I did remember! They buried a bag of, I think, fifty silver dollars. You know, outside of Nevada, Montana was one of the only places they really used silver dollars as money. Even in the 1960s, you could walk into a lot of banks and get them. That's what the prize was, all right."

"Wow. I wish we'd found those," I say.

"But what about the vigilantes' treasure?" Daphne asks the woman. "Was there some hidden treasure somewhere else?"

Another thoughtful look comes over the woman's face. "Well, dear, I do seem to remember something about that, but I think it was always a rumor. There might have been some gold or there might not have. I'm not sure we'll ever know now."

We thank the woman and say goodbye to her. Then, a little disappointed and a little relieved, we collect our shovel and walk back to camp.

Epilogue

As disappointed as Daphne and I are about not finding the treasure, we don't have time to dwell on it. The next day, Dad One and Dad Two finish their gold prospecting project, two days ahead of schedule. They crack the whip on Daphne and me to help break camp and get the OFGOV loaded. Then, we all head back to Missoula just in time for the start of seventh grade.

For the first day or two of classes, our friends bombard us with questions about the Russell art heist and our getting kidnapped. A lot of them also ask about how we found Cat, the Governor's dog. After the initial excitement of seeing friends again dies down, well...I'd be lying if I said things get back to normal. How could seventh grade ever be normal?

That especially hits home with Daphne and me. It's the first time either of us have had an official boyfriend/girlfriend at school, and well, it's kind of weird. It doesn't help that Daphne is on yearbook now. She suddenly thinks she's all cool being their new chief photographer, and we end up arguing more than ever. As for me, I don't really know what I'm supposed to be doing. I go to classes and hang out with my friends Ryan and Nick, but suddenly, I'm not seeing Daphne nearly as much as I did during the summer. Without us even saying anything to each other, it feels like we've broken up and that last summer never even happened.

But that is a story for later. Right now, Mom's calling me and Lily for dinner, and besides, there's a big Montana Grizzlies football game tomorrow. If I'm going to meet Ryan and Nick there, I've got to get a ton of chores done first. I'm pretty sure Daphne will be there, too. Maybe she'll act normal again and we can get back to how we felt over the summer.

Then again, maybe something big will happen. Something that will pull us together again. With Daphne and me, you just never know.

The End

Researching Bannack, Gold, Vigilantes, and Charles Russell

H*angman's Gold* offered me an opportunity to learn more about many of the West's most fascinating subjects, and I did my best to accurately describe and portray the people, history, places, and geology Daphne and Slate encounter. To learn about these things, I read a number of fascinating books including Frederick Allen's *A Decent Orderly Lynching: The Montana Vigilantes*; Nathaniel P. Langford's *Vigilante Days and Ways*; Thomas J. Dimsdale's *The Vigilantes of Montana*; and John Taliaferro's *Charles M. Russell: the life and legend of America's cowboy artist*. Even better, I made three research trips to Bannack and Dillon, two of them with my son and research assistant, Braden. We walked through the ghost town "collecting clues," took hundreds of photographs, checked out Dillon's hotspots, and talked to historians, tour guides, art experts, store owners, and police officers.

I did take several small liberties in recounting Slate's and Daphne's latest adventure. In the Dillon Hotel and Bar, for instance, the pay phone is actually downstairs, not upstairs. The two sheep headstones I describe in the new cemetery are also not identical—though there are two identical ones with the "bricks" behind them. And while several ghosts have been spotted in Bannack, to my knowledge, the ghost of Dorothy has not been observed sitting at a schoolroom desk.

One thing I especially would like to make clear is that Montana Historical Society in Helena and C.M. Russell Museum in Great Falls take immaculate care of their priceless Charles M. Russell collections, and would never put them in harm's way. In fact, if you get a chance to visit these two museums, as well as the University of Montana Western Gallery and Museum, I highly recommend them. Standing face-to-face with some of America's greatest works of art is not an experience you'll soon forget.

For that matter, I hope that Slate and Daphne inspire all of their fans to explore the history not only of Montana, but of your own communities. Fascinating history, people, and mystery surround us. Go out and get sleuthing!

Striking Gold

I especially have University of Montana geology professor Jim Sears to thank for inspiring this second Slate Stephens Mystery. I confess that I hadn't been thinking of choosing Bannack as a follow-up location to *The Governor's Dog is Missing*. Then, Professor Sears invited me on a field trip to the Bannack area with one of his geology classes. While showing me the complicated geology of the area, he took me to Road Agents Rock and started talking about the vigilantes and history of territorial Montana. I was so intrigued that I decided to, ahem, dig deeper. Later, Professor Sears helped explain the nuts and bolts of minerals geology and gold mining to me, as well as reviewing the final manuscript.

Essential to my research were the experts at Bannack itself. Assistant Park Manager Tom Lowe, Interpretive Ranger John Phillips, and Tour Guide Arlis Vannett were especially helpful in answering my questions, as well as allowing me into the Masonic Lodge, Bannack Mill, and the actual hardrock mine above it.

My special thanks go to Delores Morrow and Amanda Streeter at the Montana Historical Society for granting me permission to use Russell's masterpiece *Bronc to Breakfast* on the cover of Hangman's Gold. Also to Librarian Sharon McGowan at the C.M. Russell Museum for sharing her knowledge of the great artist and pointing me toward further resources. Thanks also to the staff of the University of Montana Western Gallery and Museum for answering my questions about their collection.

I am grateful to the many kind people of Dillon who made my research visits both productive and enjoyable. These include Debbie Sporich, owner of The (wonderful and amazing) Bookstore at 26 North Idaho Street in Dillon, and Patrolman Franklin D. Kluesner of the Dillon Police Department.

Preparing and publishing any book is no small project, and I have several people to thank in that regards. Big thanks to my writer's group for their comments on the early chapters, and even bigger thanks to Bruce Weide and Amy Ratzlaf for their terrific and insightful critiques of the entire manuscript. I'd also like to thank another fine writer Shelley Freese for her excellent copy-editing skills and offer to pitch in. As always, I am honored to have Kathy Herlihy-Paoli of Inkstone Design turn this project into a beautiful work of art, and Steve Isaacson keeping the Bucking Horse Books website kickin'!

Finally, I'd like to thank my family for enthusiastically supporting and helping with my latest writing adventure. My wife Amy, daughter Tessa, and son Braden are the true gold in my life.

Other Selected Titles by Sneed B. Collard III

MIDDLE-GRADE AND YOUNG ADULT FICTION
Dog Sense, winner of the ASPCA Henry Bergh Award
Flash Point, winner of the Green Earth Book Award
Double Eagle, on the state award lists for Kansas, Vermont,
    Pennsylvania, and Missouri
Slate Stephens Mysteries:
    The Governor's Dog is Missing
    Hangman's Gold

NONFICTION PICTURE BOOKS
Animal Dads
Beaks
Creepy Creatures
Our Wet World
Many Biomes, One Earth
The Forest in the Clouds
The Deep Sea Floor
A Platypus, Probably
Wings
Teeth
B is for Big Sky Country—A Montana Alphabet
Shep—Our Most Loyal Dog

NONFICTION MIDDLE-GRADE and YOUNG ADULT
The World Famous Miles City Bucking Horse Sale
Monteverde—Science and Scientists in a Costa Rican Cloud Forest
The Prairie Builders—Reconstructing America's Lost Grasslands
Pocket Babies and Other Amazing Marsupials
Science Warriors—The Battle Against Invasive Species
Reign of the Sea Dragons
Global Warming: A Personal Guide to Causes and Solutions

For the latest on Sneed Collard books, check the following:
www.sneedbcollardiii.com *and* www.buckinghorsebooks.com.